新民
说

成
为
更
好
的
人

BOB DYLAN
THE LYRICS 1961–2012
鲍勃·迪伦诗歌集

敲着天堂的大门

[美] 鲍勃·迪伦　著

冷霜　胡桑　李皖　西川　周公度　译

广西师范大学出版社

·桂林·

QIAO ZHE TIANTANG DE DAMEN

LYRICS: 1961-2012
著作权合同登记号桂图登字：20-2017-053 号

图书在版编目（CIP）数据

　鲍勃·迪伦诗歌集：1961—2012. 敲着天堂的大门：
汉英对照 /（美）鲍勃·迪伦著；冷霜等译. —桂林：
广西师范大学出版社，2017.6（2018.7 重印）
　书名原文：LYRICS：1961-2012
　ISBN 978-7-5495-9686-7

　Ⅰ. ①鲍… Ⅱ. ①鲍…②冷… Ⅲ. ①诗集-美国-
现代-汉、英 Ⅳ. ①I712.25

　中国版本图书馆 CIP 数据核字（2017）第 079140 号

出　版：广西师范大学出版社
　　　　广西桂林市五里店路 9 号　邮政编码：541004
网　址：http://www.bbtpress.com
出版人：张艺兵
发　行：广西师范大学出版社
　　　　电话：（0773）2802178
印　刷：山东临沂新华印刷物流集团有限责任公司印刷
　　　　山东临沂高新技术产业开发区新华路
　　　　邮政编码：276017
开　本：740 mm × 1 092 mm　1/32
印　张：7.5　　　字数：85 千字
版　次：2017 年 6 月第 1 版　　2018 年 7 月第 3 次
定　价：25.00 元

如发现印装质量问题，影响阅读，请与出版社发行部门联系调换。

目录

自画像

崭新的清晨

Now

there & I am waiting / to find out the price
you got to pay to get out of ~~going~~ going through everything twice

Asking some little french girl if she knows me very well

Oh Mister / This could be the end
(and) in Mobile with —
stuck in

自画像
Self Portrait

冷霜 译

　　《自画像》是鲍勃·迪伦的第十张录音室专辑，1970年6月8日由哥伦比亚唱片公司发行。这是迪伦继《金发叠金发》之后的第二张双唱片专辑，收录了很多著名流行歌曲和民谣的翻唱，也有少量器乐曲和原创作品。其中绝大多数歌曲都以迪伦一年前在《纳什维尔天际线》中所引入的、受乡村音乐影响的哼吟式唱腔演唱。

　　此专辑与迪伦以往作品差异颇大，面世后在乐评界引起了巨大争议。其有意为之的超现实风格和时不时的尖刻口吻，招致了非常极端的批评，如美国乐评家格雷尔·马库斯（Greil Marcus）就曾在《滚石》杂志上撰文讥之。尽管如此，这张专辑还是受到了公众的热捧，在美国迅速成为畅销唱片，一度登上《公告牌》专辑榜第四名，在英国更是位列单曲排行榜榜首，其中的一些歌曲后来被不断翻唱或出现在电影里。直至2013年，《靴子腿第十辑：另一个自画像（1969—1971）》发行后，这张专辑才重新获得了肯定性的评价。

迪伦在接受采访时声称这张专辑是他开的一个玩笑,以此甩掉那些追随在他身后的人群以及"一代人的代言人"这一标签。不过,在克诺夫(Knopf)出版社于 1973 年出版的名为《作品与草图》(*Writings and Drawings*)的迪伦歌词、速写、笔记集,以及在此基础上分别于 1985 年、2000 年增订再版的歌词集里,均未收入《自画像》中的原创歌词,只有《忧伤地活着》和《吟游男孩》两首被收入《纳什维尔天际线》的附加歌词之中。这在一定程度上,也表明了迪伦当时对这张专辑并不认可。直到 2004 年的新版,它们才以单行专辑的形式被收入其中。本书亦只收录了此专辑中《忧伤地活着》《吟游男孩》两首原创作品。

冷霜

忧伤地活着

自从你离开
我一直在徘徊
冲着鞋子耷拉着脑袋
我忧伤地度过
没有你的每一个夜晚

我不用走得很远
去知道你在哪里
陌生人都给了我消息
我忧伤地度过
没有你的每一个夜晚

我想我最好
立刻去休息
并忘记我的骄傲
可我却抵挡不了
我心底为你
盛着的这份情感

你若看到我这样

你会回来你也会留下
哦，你怎么能拒绝
我已忧伤地度过
没有你的每一个夜晚

Living the Blues

Since you've been gone
I've been walking around
With my head bowed down to my shoes
I've been living the blues
Ev'ry night without you

I don't have to go far
To know where you are
Strangers all give me the news
I've been living the blues
Ev'ry night without you

I think that it's best
I soon get some rest
And forget my pride
But I can't deny
This feeling that I
Carry for you deep down inside

If you see me this way
You'd come back and you'd stay
Oh, how could you refuse
I've been living the blues
Ev'ry night without you

吟游男孩

谁会扔给那吟游男孩一枚硬币？
谁会让它滚动？
谁会扔给那吟游男孩一枚硬币？
谁会让它轻松落下拯救他灵魂？

哦，拉凯[1]已驾驶很长很长时间
如今他被卡在山顶
用十二个前进挡，经过漫长艰苦的攀登
和所有那些女士一起，然而，他仍旧孤单

谁会扔给那吟游男孩一枚硬币？
谁会让它滚动？
谁会扔给那吟游男孩一枚硬币？
谁会让它轻松落下拯救他灵魂？

唉，他深陷于数字而疲于劳碌
强大的反舌鸟，他仍有如此的重负
低于他的限度，对于他所有的旅行

---

1. 拉凯（Lucky）的名字意为"幸运的"。

我还能多说什么，而我还在那条路上

谁会扔给那吟游男孩一枚硬币？
谁会让它滚动？
谁会扔给那吟游男孩一枚硬币？
谁会让它轻松落下拯救他灵魂？

Minstrel Boy

Who's gonna throw that minstrel boy a coin?
Who's gonna let it roll?
Who's gonna throw that minstrel boy a coin?
Who's gonna let it down easy to save his soul?

Oh, Lucky's been drivin' a long, long time
And now he's stuck on top of the hill
With twelve forward gears, it's been a long hard climb
And with all of them ladies, though, he's lonely still

Who's gonna throw that minstrel boy a coin?
Who's gonna let it roll?
Who's gonna throw that minstrel boy a coin?
Who's gonna let it down easy to save his soul?

Well, he deep in number and heavy in toil
Mighty Mockingbird, he still has such a heavy load
Beneath his bound'ries, what more can I tell
With all of his trav'lin', but I'm still on that road

Who's gonna throw that minstrel boy a coin?
Who's gonna let it roll?
Who's gonna throw that minstrel boy a coin?
Who's gonna let it down easy to save his soul?

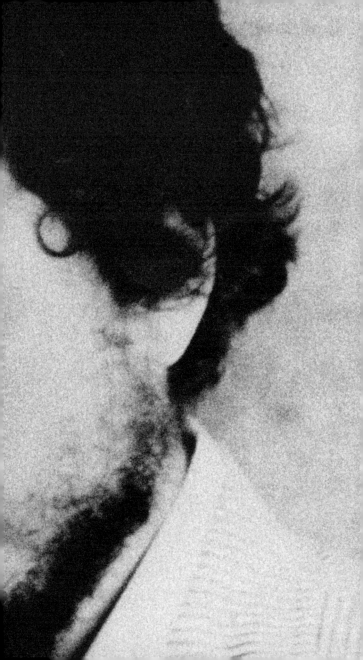

BIRD ON THE HORIZON, SITTING ON A FENCE
He's singing his song for me at his own expence
And I'm just like that Bird
Oh singing just for you
I hope that you can hear
HEAR ME singing thru these tears

崭新的清晨
New Morning

胡桑　译

　　《崭新的清晨》是鲍勃·迪伦的第十一张专辑，1970 年 10 月由哥伦比亚唱片公司发行。这时距离上一张专辑《自画像》的面世仅仅四个月，事实上，里面的许多歌曲完成于《自画像》发行之前。

　　歌迷与乐评家对这张专辑均给予了好评，对其中带着鼻音的唱腔的回归尤为赞赏。面世不久后，它便登上了《公告牌》专辑榜第七名。

　　专辑名称来自迪伦为美国诗人阿齐博尔德·麦克利什（Archibald MacLeish）的音乐剧《魔鬼》（Scratch）所写的其中一首歌。他们俩相识于 1969 年，迪伦在自传《编年史：第一卷》（Chronicles: Volume One）中也讲述了这次合作。除《崭新的清晨》外，《夜晚的父》《时间缓缓流逝》也是专为这部音乐剧创作的。随之而来的严肃思考，让该专辑中不少歌曲都带有庄严的场景感和宗教气息。

与此同时，歌中又可见路上的野兔和土拨鼠、桥下溪流里的鱼、夜空中的星星、破晓时的鸡鸣，描绘出乡间生活的轻松惬快，迪伦对此颇为满意，自言不同以往，这些歌曲的旨趣并无甚特别寓意。虽然如此，歌词里仍多少隐藏着其人生轨迹：《去见吉普赛人》的背后是面对偶像"猫王"时内心的忐忑焦虑，《我身体里的男人》赞颂自己的贤内助萨拉（Sara Dylan），《蝗虫之日》则在抒发被普林斯顿大学授予荣誉博士头衔的微妙感受。

　　迪伦的这张专辑，看似黯淡而感伤，却回归至昔日的自我，从崭新的清晨，再度出发。

胡桑

若非为你

若非为你
宝贝，我无法找到门口
甚至看不到地板
我将悲伤忧郁
若非为你

若非为你
宝贝，我将整夜无眠
等待黎明的曙光
照耀进来
但那也不会是新鲜事物
若非为你

若非为你
我的天空会塌陷
雨水也将积聚
没有你的爱我无处安身
若非为你，我将迷失
而你知道，这是真的

若非为你
我的天空会塌陷
雨水也将积聚
没有你的爱我无处安身
哦！我该怎么办
若非为你

若非为你
冬日之后不再是春天
听不到知更鸟的吟唱
我摸不着头绪
反正听起来不真实
若非为你

If Not for You

If not for you
Babe, I couldn't find the door
Couldn't even see the floor
I'd be sad and blue
If not for you

If not for you
Babe, I'd lay awake all night
Wait for the mornin' light
To shine in through
But it would not be new
If not for you

If not for you
My sky would fall
Rain would gather too
Without your love I'd be nowhere at all
I'd be lost if not for you
And you know it's true

If not for you
My sky would fall
Rain would gather too
Without your love I'd be nowhere at all
Oh! what would I do
If not for you

If not for you
Winter would have no spring

Couldn't hear the robin sing
I just wouldn't have a clue
Anyway it wouldn't ring true
If not for you

蝗虫之日 [1]

哦，长椅沾染了眼泪和汗水

群鸟从一棵树飞到另一棵

无话可说，没有交谈

当我走上台去领我的学位证书

而蝗虫在远处吟唱

是的，蝗虫唱着如此甜蜜的旋律

哦，蝗虫在远处吟唱

是的，蝗虫在吟唱，它们为我而歌

我瞥了一眼会议室，法官们在那里谈话

黑暗弥漫四周，闻上去像一个坟墓

我准备离开，我已经移步

但紧接着我看到房间里有一道光

而蝗虫唱着，是的，这让我打了个冷战

哦，蝗虫唱着如此甜蜜的旋律

哦，蝗虫高声吟唱，声音哀伤而颤抖

---

1. 蝗虫之日，源自美国作家纳撒尼尔·韦斯特（Nathanael West）的同名小说，小说名源出《圣经》，如《旧约·出埃及记》10，耶和华使埃及出现蝗灾。

是的，蝗虫在吟唱，它们为我而歌

大门外，卡车正在卸货
天气很热，接近 90 度 [1]
那人站在我身旁，他的脑袋爆炸了
好吧，我在祈求碎片不要落在我身上
是的，蝗虫在远处吟唱
是的，蝗虫唱着如此甜蜜的旋律
哦，蝗虫在远处吟唱
蝗虫在吟唱，它们为我而歌

我脱下礼服，拿起我的证书
紧抱着我心爱的人，我们开车离去
笔直去往山里，达科他的黑色群山
当然，我们很高兴活着离开那里
而蝗虫唱着，好吧，这让我打了个冷战
是的，蝗虫唱着如此甜蜜的旋律
蝗虫高声吟唱，声音哀伤而颤抖
是的，蝗虫在吟唱，它们为我而歌
为我而歌，好吧，为我而歌

---

1. 华氏 90 度约为摄氏 32.2 度。

Day of the Locusts

Oh, the benches were stained with tears and perspiration
The birdies were flying from tree to tree
There was little to say, there was no conversation
As I stepped to the stage to pick up my degree
And the locusts sang off in the distance
Yeah, the locusts sang such a sweet melody
Oh, the locusts sang off in the distance
Yeah, the locusts sang and they were singing for me

I glanced into the chamber where the judges were talking
Darkness was everywhere, it smelled like a tomb
I was ready to leave, I was already walkin'
But the next time I looked there was light in the room
And the locusts sang, yeah, it give me a chill
Oh, the locusts sang such a sweet melody
Oh, the locusts sang their high whining trill
Yeah, the locusts sang and they were singing for me

Outside of the gates the trucks were unloadin'
The weather was hot, a-nearly 90 degrees
The man standin' next to me, his head was exploding
Well, I was prayin' the pieces wouldn't fall on me
Yeah, the locusts sang off in the distance
Yeah, the locusts sang such a sweet melody
Oh, the locusts sang off in the distance
And the locusts sang and they were singing for me

I put down my robe, picked up my diploma
Took hold of my sweetheart and away we did drive

Straight for the hills, the black hills of Dakota
Sure was glad to get out of there alive
And the locusts sang, well, it give me a chill
Yeah, the locusts sang such a sweet melody
And the locusts sang with a high whinin' trill
Yeah, the locusts sang and they was singing for me
Singing for me, well, singing for me

时间缓缓流逝

时间缓缓流逝，在这里，在群山之间
我们坐在桥边，走在泉畔
捕捉野鱼，它们漂游于小溪
时间缓缓流逝，当你迷失在梦里

我曾有一个心爱的人，她人好，又漂亮
她妈妈做饭的时候，我们就坐在厨房
透过窗户凝望高高在上的星辰
时间缓缓流逝，当你追寻着爱情

没有理由乘四轮马车去镇里
没有理由去集市
没有理由走向高处，没有理由走向低处
没有理由去往何处

在这里，时间在日光下缓缓流逝
我们目视前方，为保持正确的方向而努力
就像夏日的红玫瑰绽放在白日
时间缓缓流逝，渐渐消失

Time Passes Slowly

Time passes slowly up here in the mountains
We sit beside bridges and walk beside fountains
Catch the wild fishes that float through the stream
Time passes slowly when you're lost in a dream

Once I had a sweetheart, she was fine and good-lookin'
We sat in her kitchen while her mama was cookin'
Stared out the window to the stars high above
Time passes slowly when you're searchin' for love

Ain't no reason to go in a wagon to town
Ain't no reason to go to the fair
Ain't no reason to go up, ain't no reason to go down
Ain't no reason to go anywhere

Time passes slowly up here in the daylight
We stare straight ahead and try so hard to stay right
Like the red rose of summer that blooms in the day
Time passes slowly and fades away

去见吉普赛人

去见吉普赛人
在一家大酒店
看见我走来，他笑了
他说："好吧，好吧，好吧"
他的房间昏暗而拥挤
灯光微弱暗淡
"你好吗？"他对我说
我也如是问候

我下到大厅
打了一个简短的电话
一个漂亮的舞女在那里
她开始喊
"回去见那个吉普赛人
他能在背后移动你
驱使你远离恐惧
带你穿过镜子
他在拉斯维加斯做过
他在这里也可以做到"

外面灯光闪耀

在泪水之河上

我遥望着它们

音乐萦绕耳畔

我回去见到那个吉普赛人

已近破晓时分

吉普赛人的门口敞开着

但吉普赛人已离去

那个漂亮的舞女

也不见踪影

我便看着太阳升起

自那个明尼苏达州的小镇

Went to See the Gypsy

Went to see the gypsy
Stayin' in a big hotel
He smiled when he saw me coming
And he said, "Well, well, well"
His room was dark and crowded
Lights were low and dim
"How are you?" he said to me
I said it back to him

I went down to the lobby
To make a small call out
A pretty dancing girl was there
And she began to shout
"Go on back to see the gypsy
He can move you from the rear
Drive you from your fear
Bring you through the mirror
He did it in Las Vegas
And he can do it here"

Outside the lights were shining
On the river of tears
I watched them from the distance
With music in my ears

I went back to see the gypsy
It was nearly early dawn
The gypsy's door was open wide
But the gypsy was gone

And that pretty dancing girl
She could not be found
So I watched that sun come rising
From that little Minnesota town

温特露德 [1]

温特露德，温特露德，哦，亲爱的
温特露德今晚就在路边
今晚不会有争吵
一切都会好好的
哦，透过身旁的天使，我看到
爱情有着闪耀的缘由
你是我所钟爱的，来这里，给我更多
那么，温特露德，这家伙觉得你很好

温特露德，温特露德，我的小苹果
温特露德就在田野里的玉米旁
温特露德，让我们去到小教堂
然后回来，煮一顿饭吃
好吧，出来，当溜冰场在阳光下
闪着光，在老十字路口标志旁
雪那么冷，但我们的爱可以炽热
温特露德，不要太粗鲁，请属于我

---

1. 温特露德（Winterlude），女性名字，迪伦在此将"冬日"（winter）与"插曲"（interlude）合成为一个词。

温特露德，温特露德，我的小雏菊

温特露德在电话线旁

温特露德，让我慵懒

来吧，坐柴火旁

窗子映着月色

雪花，覆盖了沙地

出来吧今晚，一切都会是紧凑的

温特露德，这家伙觉得你很棒

Winterlude

Winterlude, Winterlude, oh darlin'
Winterlude by the road tonight
Tonight there will be no quarrelin'
Ev'rything is gonna be all right
Oh, I see by the angel beside me
That love has a reason to shine
You're the one I adore, come over here and give me more
Then Winterlude, this dude thinks you're fine

Winterlude, Winterlude, my little apple
Winterlude by the corn in the field
Winterlude, let's go down to the chapel
Then come back and cook up a meal
Well, come out when the skating rink glistens
By the sun, near the old crossroads sign
The snow is so cold, but our love can be bold
Winterlude, don't be rude, please be mine

Winterlude, Winterlude, my little daisy
Winterlude by the telephone wire
Winterlude, it's makin' me lazy
Come on, sit by the logs in the fire
The moonlight reflects from the window
Where the snowflakes, they cover the sand
Come out tonight, ev'rything will be tight
Winterlude, this dude thinks you're grand

要是狗都自由奔跑

要是狗都自由奔跑，那我们为何不
穿越陡斜的平原？
我的耳畔听到一首
两头骡子、火车和雨的交响乐
最好的总是在来的路上
他们这样对我解释
干好你的事，你将会是国王
要是狗都自由奔跑

要是狗都自由奔跑，我为何不
穿越时间的沼泽？
我的脑海编织着一首交响乐
和韵律的织锦
哦，风把我的故事吹向你
所以它可以飘扬，成为
每个人自己的故事，这都无从知晓
要是狗都自由奔跑

要是狗都自由奔跑，那必须如此的
就必须如此，就是这样

真爱可以让草叶

笔直高耸

与浩瀚的海融为一体

真爱无需陪伴

它可以治愈灵魂，让灵魂变得完整

要是狗都自由奔跑

If Dogs Run Free

If dogs run free, then why not we
Across the swooping plain?
My ears hear a symphony
Of two mules, trains and rain
The best is always yet to come
That's what they explain to me
Just do your thing, you'll be king
If dogs run free

If dogs run free, why not me
Across the swamp of time?
My mind weaves a symphony
And tapestry of rhyme
Oh, winds which rush my tale to thee
So it may flow and be
To each his own, it's all unknown
If dogs run free

If dogs run free, then what must be
Must be, and that is all
True love can make a blade of grass
Stand up straight and tall
In harmony with the cosmic sea
True love needs no company
It can cure the soul, it can make it whole
If dogs run free

崭新的清晨

你没听到公鸡的啼叫？
兔子飞奔穿过马路
桥的下面，水潺潺流过
多么高兴，只要看到你的笑容
在蔚蓝的天空之下
在这崭新的清晨，崭新的清晨
在这和你一起的崭新的清晨

你没听到马达的发动？
汽车正流行起来
沿着公路开一两段远路
多么高兴，只要看到你的笑容
在蔚蓝的天空之下
在这崭新的清晨，崭新的清晨
在这和你一起的崭新的清晨

夜晚稍纵即逝
它总是这样，当我和你在一起

你没感觉到太阳闪耀的光芒？

土拨鼠沿着乡间的溪流奔跑

这一定是我所有梦想成真的那一天

只要活着，就很幸福

在蔚蓝的天空之下

在这崭新的清晨，崭新的清晨

在这和你一起的崭新的清晨

只要活着，就很幸福

在蔚蓝的天空之下

在这崭新的清晨，崭新的清晨

在这和你一起的崭新的清晨

崭新的清晨……

New Morning

Can't you hear that rooster crowin'?
Rabbit runnin' down across the road
Underneath the bridge where the water flowed through
So happy just to see you smile
Underneath the sky of blue
On this new morning, new morning
On this new morning with you

Can't you hear that motor turnin'?
Automobile comin' into style
Comin' down the road for a country mile or two
So happy just to see you smile
Underneath the sky of blue
On this new morning, new morning
On this new morning with you

The night passed away so quickly
It always does when you're with me

Can't you feel that sun a-shinin'?
Groundhog runnin' by the country stream
This must be the day that all of my dreams come true
So happy just to be alive
Underneath the sky of blue
On this new morning, new morning
On this new morning with you

So happy just to be alive
Underneath the sky of blue

On this new morning, new morning
On this new morning with you
New morning…

窗户上的标识

窗户上的标识写着"孤独"

门上的标识写着"禁止陪伴"

街上的标识写着"我不归你"

门廊上的标识写着"三人太挤"[1]

门廊上的标识写着"三人太挤"

她和男朋友去了加利福尼亚

她和男朋友变换了心情

我最好的朋友说:"喏,我没警告过你吗

布莱顿姑娘就像月亮

布莱顿姑娘就像月亮"

看来只是有雨……

今晚的主街肯定会一片湿漉漉……

希望冰雹不要落下

给我造一所小屋子,在犹他州

给我娶一位妻子,一起钓虹鳟鱼

———————

1. 三人太挤,出自谚语"两人成伴,三人不欢"。

有一堆孩子，喊我"爸爸"

这必定就是所有的一切

这必定就是所有的一切

Sign on the Window

Sign on the window says "Lonely"
Sign on the door said "No Company Allowed"
Sign on the street says "Y' Don't Own Me"
Sign on the porch says "Three's A Crowd"
Sign on the porch says "Three's A Crowd"

Her and her boyfriend went to California
Her and her boyfriend done changed their tune
My best friend said, "Now didn' I warn ya
Brighton girls are like the moon
Brighton girls are like the moon"

Looks like a-nothing but rain…
Sure gonna be wet tonight on Main Street…
Hope that it don't sleet

Build me a cabin in Utah
Marry me a wife, catch rainbow trout
Have a bunch of kids who call me "Pa"
That must be what it's all about
That must be what it's all about

又一个周末

溜来滑去，像一只逃窜的鼹鼠
我多么希望见到你，是的，我们可以找些乐子
又一个周末，又一个与你一起的周末
又一个周末，又一个周末将会到来

来我的船上，宝贝，登上甲板
我们将飞过海洋，正如你所猜想的
又一个周末，又一个与你一起的周末
又一个周末，又一个周末将会到来

我们将放飞夜晚
次日出去玩整整一天
一切都会很好
你等着看
我们将去某个未知的地方
把所有的孩子留在家中
亲爱的，何不就我们自己离开
就你和我

来来回回，就像丛林里的兔子

只要见到你我就高兴，是啊，多么地希望

又一个周末，又一个与你一起的周末

又一个周末，又一个周末将会到来（是的，你会的！）

便是草垛里的一根针，我也要把你找到

你是这个男孩能得到的最甜蜜的出走妈妈 [1]

又一个周末，又一个与你一起的周末

又一个周末，又一个周末将会到来

---

1. 妈妈，口语中又有"情人""妻子"之意。

One More Weekend

Slippin' and slidin' like a weasel on the run
I'm lookin' good to see you, yeah, and we can have some fun
One more weekend, one more weekend with you
One more weekend, one more weekend'll do

Come on down to my ship, honey, ride on deck
We'll fly over the ocean just like you suspect
One more weekend, one more weekend with you
One more weekend, one more weekend'll do

We'll fly the night away
Hang out the whole next day
Things will be okay
You wait and see
We'll go someplace unknown
Leave all the children home
Honey, why not go alone
Just you and me

Comin' and goin' like a rabbit in the wood
I'm happy just to see you, yeah, lookin' so good
One more weekend, one more weekend with you
One more weekend, one more weekend'll do (yes, you will!)

Like a needle in a haystack, I'm gonna find you yet
You're the sweetest gone mama that this boy's ever gonna
   get
One more weekend, one more weekend with you
One more weekend, one more weekend'll do

我身体里的男人

我身体里的男人几乎能完成任何工作
对于酬劳，几乎一无所求
找一个像你一样的女人
来理解我身体里的男人

暴风云在我的门外肆虐
我告诉自己我无法继续承受
找一个像你这样的女人
来发现我身体里的男人

但是，哦，多么美妙的感觉
只要知道你在近旁
我的心一阵悸动
从脚趾直达耳朵

我身体里的男人有时会躲起来，不让看见
那只是因为他不想变成某种机器
找一个像你一样的女人
来理解我身体里的男人

The Man in Me

The man in me will do nearly any task
And as for compensation, there's little he would ask
Take a woman like you
To get through to the man in me

Storm clouds are raging all around my door
I think to myself I might not take it anymore
Take a woman like your kind
To find the man in me

But, oh, what a wonderful feeling
Just to know that you are near
Sets my heart a-reeling
From my toes up to my ears

The man in me will hide sometimes to keep from bein' seen
But that's just because he doesn't want to turn into some
    machine
Took a woman like you
To get through to the man in me

三个天使

三个天使在街道上空

每一个都吹着号角

穿着绿色的长袍，翅膀从中舒展

自从圣诞节的早晨，他们就在那里

来自蒙大拿的最狂野的猫一闪而过

接着是一位身穿亮丽橘色裙子的女士

一辆搬运拖车，一辆没有轮子的卡车

第十大道的巴士向西驶去

狗和鸽子飞起来，它们四处扑腾

一个戴徽章的男人匆匆溜过

三个小伙子迟缓地走在回去工作的路上

无人停下问为什么

面包店的卡车停在栅栏的外面

天使们高高驻足于栅栏的尖上

司机往外窥视，想找到一张脸

在这遍布灵魂的混凝土世界

天使们整天都在吹着号角

运行中的整个地球似乎要经过

但有人听到天使们演奏的音乐吗

有人试着去听吗？

Three Angels

Three angels up above the street
Each one playing a horn
Dressed in green robes with wings that stick out
They've been there since Christmas morn
The wildest cat from Montana passes by in a flash
Then a lady in a bright orange dress
One U-Haul trailer, a truck with no wheels
The Tenth Avenue bus going west
The dogs and pigeons fly up and they flutter around
A man with a badge skips by
Three fellas crawlin' on their way back to work
Nobody stops to ask why
The bakery truck stops outside of that fence
Where the angels stand high on their poles
The driver peeks out, trying to find one face
In this concrete world full of souls
The angels play on their horns all day
The whole earth in progression seems to pass by
But does anyone hear the music they play
Does anyone even try?

夜晚的父

夜晚的父，白昼的父
父啊，将黑暗驱散的那位
父啊，教鸟儿飞翔的那位
在天空搭建彩虹的那位
孤独与痛苦的父
爱的父，雨的父

白昼的父，夜晚的父
黑的父，白的父
父啊，将山造得如此高的那位
为空中的云朵赋形的那位
时间的父，梦的父
父啊，让江河和溪流转向的那位

谷物的父，小麦的父
冷的父，热的父
空气的父，树木的父
栖居于我们的心和记忆中的那位
时刻的父，岁月的父
我们致以最庄重的赞美的父

Father of Night

Father of night, Father of day
Father, who taketh the darkness away
Father, who teacheth the bird to fly
Builder of rainbows up in the sky
Father of loneliness and pain
Father of love and Father of rain

Father of day, Father of night
Father of black, Father of white
Father, who build the mountain so high
Who shapeth the cloud up in the sky
Father of time, Father of dreams
Father, who turneth the rivers and streams

Father of grain, Father of wheat
Father of cold and Father of heat
Father of air and Father of trees
Who dwells in our hearts and our memories
Father of minutes, Father of days
Father of whom we most solemnly praise

时刻想要拥有你

（与乔治·哈里森合作）

让我进来，我知道我已在这里

让我进入你心里

让我了解你，让我展现给你

让我高声唱给你

我所有的一切都是你的

你看到的一切都是我的

我如此高兴能拥你入怀

时刻想要拥有你

让我说出，让我表演

让我给你出主意

让我了解你，让我展现给你

让它在你身上成长

我所有的一切都是你的

你看到的一切都是我的

我如此高兴能拥你入怀

时刻想要拥有你

让我进来，我知道我已在这里

让我进入你心里

让我了解你，让我展现给你

让我高声唱给你

我所有的一切都是你的

你看到的一切都是我的

我如此高兴能拥你入怀

时刻想要拥有你

I'd Have You Any Time
(with George Harrison)

Let me in here, I know I've been here
Let me into your heart
Let me know you, let me show you
Let me roll it to you
All I have is yours
All you see is mine
And I'm glad to have you in my arms
I'd have you any time

Let me say it, let me play it
Let me lay it on you
Let me know you, let me show you
Let me grow it on you
All I have is yours
All you see is mine
And I'm glad to have you in my arms
I'd have you any time

Let me in here, I know I've been here
Let me into your heart
Let me know you, let me show you
Let me roll it to you
All I have is yours
All you see is mine
And I'm glad to have you in my arms
I'd have you any time

望着河水流淌

我身上发生了什么
我没太多话可说
阳光潜入窗子
我仍旧在这间通宵咖啡馆
在月光下来来回回走动
出去外面，卡车缓缓开过
在这沙堤上坐下来
望着河水流淌

希望我回到了城市
而不是在这老旧的沙堤
阳光直射在烟囱顶上
我所爱的人近在咫尺
假如我有翅膀，可以飞翔
我知道自己要去哪里
但此刻，我就坐在这里，心满意足
望着河水流淌

人们在关于一切的一切上都意见纷纭，是的
让你停下，都想知道为什么

为何就在昨天我看到有人在街上

禁不住哭泣呢

哦，但这条古老的河翻流不息

不在乎路上有什么，也不关心风从何方吹来

只要它依旧如故，我就坐在这里

望着河水流淌

所见之处人们意见纷纭

让你想要停下来，读一本书

为何就在昨天我看到有人在街上

真的很吓人呢

但这条古老的河翻流不息

不在乎路上有什么，也不关心风从何方吹来

只要它依旧如故，我就坐在这里

望着河水流淌

望着河水流淌

望着河水流淌

望着河水流淌

但我要在这沙堤上坐下来

望着河水流淌

Watching the River Flow

What's the matter with me
I don't have much to say
Daylight sneakin' through the window
And I'm still in this all-night café
Walkin' to and fro beneath the moon
Out to where the trucks are rollin' slow
To sit down on this bank of sand
And watch the river flow

Wish I was back in the city
Instead of this old bank of sand
With the sun beating down over the chimney tops
And the one I love so close at hand
If I had wings and I could fly
I know where I would go
But right now I'll just sit here so contentedly
And watch the river flow

People disagreeing on all just about everything, yeah
Makes you stop and all wonder why
Why only yesterday I saw somebody on the street
Who just couldn't help but cry
Oh, this ol' river keeps on rollin', though
No matter what gets in the way and which way the wind
   does blow
And as long as it does I'll just sit here
And watch the river flow

People disagreeing everywhere you look

Makes you wanna stop and read a book
Why only yesterday I saw somebody on the street
That was really shook
But this ol' river keeps on rollin', though
No matter what gets in the way and which way the wind
   does blow
And as long as it does I'll just sit here
And watch the river flow

Watch the river flow
Watchin' the river flow
Watchin' the river flow
But I'll sit down on this bank of sand
And watch the river flow

当我画下我的杰作

哦，罗马的街道满是碎石

古老的足迹遍布各处

你几乎会觉得自己看到了两个世界

在一个寒冷、黑暗的夜晚，在西班牙阶梯[1]上

匆匆忙忙回到酒店房间

那里，我约了波提切利的侄女

她答应会在那里陪我一起

当我画下我的杰作

哦，在斗兽场内度过的时辰

躲避狮子，虚掷光阴

哦，这些强健有力的丛林之王，看见它们我几乎无法站立

是的，确实是一段漫长、艰辛的攀援

火车车轮碾过我记忆的背部

当我在山顶跟着一群野鹅奔跑

有朝一日，一切都将如狂想曲般流畅

当我画下我的杰作

---

1. 西班牙阶梯，即意大利罗马的西班牙大台阶，连接山上天主圣三教堂与西班牙广场的户外阶梯。

乘着一艘肮脏的贡多拉四处漫游
哦，回到可口可乐的世界！

我离开罗马，抵达布鲁塞尔
乘坐的飞机如此颠簸，几乎将我弄哭
穿着制服的牧师和肌肉发达的姑娘
当我步入，每个人都在向我问候
吃着糖果的新闻记者
必定被大块头的警察制止
有朝一日，一切都会变得不同
当我画下我的杰作

When I Paint My Masterpiece

Oh, the streets of Rome are filled with rubble
Ancient footprints are everywhere
You can almost think that you're seein' double
On a cold, dark night on the Spanish Stairs
Got to hurry on back to my hotel room
Where I've got me a date with Botticelli's niece
She promised that she'd be right there with me
When I paint my masterpiece

Oh, the hours I've spent inside the Coliseum
Dodging lions and wastin' time
Oh, those mighty kings of the jungle, I could hardly stand
    to see 'em
Yes, it sure has been a long, hard climb
Train wheels runnin' through the back of my memory
When I ran on the hilltop following a pack of wild geese
Someday, everything is gonna be smooth like a rhapsody
When I paint my masterpiece

Sailin' round the world in a dirty gondola
Oh, to be back in the land of Coca-Cola!

I left Rome and landed in Brussels
On a plane ride so bumpy that I almost cried
Clergymen in uniform and young girls pullin' muscles
Everyone was there to greet me when I stepped inside
Newspapermen eating candy
Had to be held down by big police
Someday, everything is gonna be diff'rent
When I paint my masterpiece

壁花

壁花，壁花
你不和我一起跳舞吗？
我也伤心寂寞
壁花，壁花
你不和我一起跳舞吗？
我正在爱上你

像你一样，我也想知道自己在这里做什么
像你一样，我也想知道怎么回事

壁花，壁花
你不想和我一起跳舞吗？
夜晚很快就会过去

我看到你站在缭绕的烟雾中
我知道，你将成为我的，就在这些天
只属于我

壁花，壁花
给我一个机会
请让我载你回家

Wallflower

Wallflower, wallflower
Won't you dance with me?
I'm sad and lonely too
Wallflower, wallflower
Won't you dance with me?
I'm fallin' in love with you

Just like you I'm wondrin' what I'm doin' here
Just like you I'm wondrin' what's goin' on

Wallflower, wallflower
Won't you dance with me?
The night will soon be gone

I have seen you standing in the smoky haze
And I know that you're gonna be mine one of these days
Mine alone

Wallflower, wallflower
Take a chance on me
Please let me ride you home

乔治·杰克逊 [1]

清晨我醒来

床上残存着泪水

他们杀死了一个我真心所爱的人

一枪射穿脑袋

天啊，天啊

他们杀死了乔治·杰克逊

天啊，天啊

他们将他埋入地下

将他送入监狱

因为抢劫了七十美元

门在他身后关上

他们丢掉了钥匙

天啊，天啊

他们杀死了乔治·杰克逊

天啊，天啊

他们将他埋入地下

---

1. 乔治·杰克逊（George Jackson，1941—1971），美国黑豹党成员，1971 年 8 月 21 日在美国加利福尼亚州圣昆廷监狱内因越狱而被枪杀。

他不会对任何人忍气吞声
他不会卑躬屈膝
当权者，他们恨他
因为他太过真实
天啊，天啊
他们杀死了乔治·杰克逊
天啊，天啊
他们将他埋在地下

那些狱警，他们咒骂他
从高处监视他
但他们惧怕他的力量
他们惊恐于他的爱
天啊，天啊
因此他们杀死了乔治·杰克逊
天啊，天啊
他们将他埋入地下

有时我觉得这整个世界
就是一个巨大监狱的院子
我们中的有些人是囚犯
其他的是狱警
天啊，天啊

他们杀死了乔治·杰克逊

天啊，天啊

他们将他埋入地下

George Jackson

I woke up this mornin'
There were tears in my bed
They killed a man I really loved
Shot him through the head
Lord, Lord
They cut George Jackson down
Lord, Lord
They laid him in the ground

Sent him off to prison
For a seventy-dollar robbery
Closed the door behind him
And they threw away the key
Lord, Lord
They cut George Jackson down
Lord, Lord
They laid him in the ground

He wouldn't take shit from no one
He wouldn't bow down or kneel
Authorities, they hated him
Because he was just too real
Lord, Lord
They cut George Jackson down
Lord, Lord
They laid him in the ground

Prison guards, they cursed him
As they watched him from above

But they were frightened of his power
They were scared of his love
Lord, Lord
So they cut George Jackson down
Lord, Lord
They laid him in the ground

Sometimes I think this whole world
Is one big prison yard
Some of us are prisoners
The rest of us are guards
Lord, Lord
They cut George Jackson down
Lord, Lord
They laid him in the ground

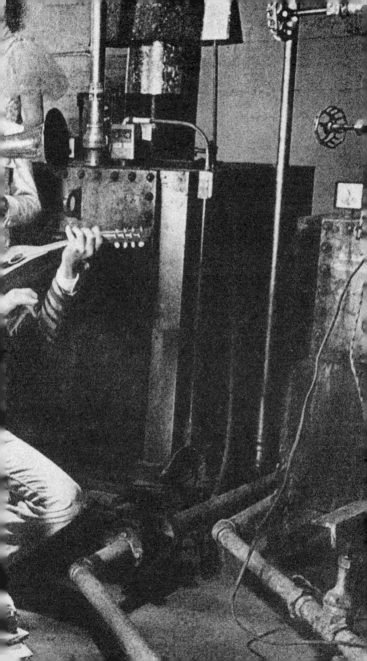

like a poor fool in his prime/trying to read your portrait
you can hear me talk

is your heart made of stone/
                             or solid rock?

got fourteen fevers and five believers all dressed up ~~littttt~~ *so fine*
tell your mama and poppa not to worry cause theyre friends of mine

dressed up like men

THE BASEMENT TAPES

地下室录音带
The Basement Tapes

李皖　译（郝佳　校）

　　此专辑中的歌曲写于迪伦遭遇摩托车事故后的隐居时期。1967 年夏天，在租来的乡村楼房"大粉"（Big Pink）的地下室里，迪伦和"乐队"（The Band）随便玩玩，录了大约一百首歌，有民歌，也有原创歌曲。部分录音先是在音乐家朋友中流传，一些曲目经翻唱甚至走红；然后，一部分录音流传至公众中。随着时间的推移，愈来愈多的地下室录音浮出水面。1975 年 6 月 26 日，二十四首歌曲第一次以专辑形式、以《地下室录音带》为名，正式发行。

　　在英语传统民谣中，一直深埋着一些深沉、黑暗、不乏神秘的歌曲，往往以口耳相传的奇案、怪人、异事为题材。迪伦以之为源泉、为动机，联系着美国记忆、民族心理、时代动荡，在完全私密、放松和自由的状态下，改造和重写传统，创作出这一系列颇具古老英语民谣风格的歌曲。它们是狂欢式的、装疯卖傻的，又是祭典、寓言、启示录式的。

收录在此专辑中的歌词，包括了 1975 年同名专辑中迪伦创作的十八首，以及散落在其他出版物中的六首迪伦之作。

美国乐评家格雷尔·马库斯曾以《老美国志异》(*The Old, Weird America*) 为名，写了整整一本书来评论这些歌曲。在他看来，它们奇异，有种未完成的感觉，"仿佛是位于忏悔室与妓院之间"，"既富于历史意义，同时又自成机杼"。假如把这些录音标上 1881、1932、1954、1967、1992 诸如此类随便一个年份，听者同样也会信服。马库斯说，这些歌曲像是一种本能的实验，一个神秘的实验室，是"美国文化语言复苏与再创造的矿床"。其中"有一个未被发现的国度，如同日常的视野里隐藏着偷窃而来的密函"，"若干来自远古的世界亦如幽灵般重现，下定决心借尸还魂"。

李晗

鸡零狗碎

我计划好了一切并就位
你却处处违背诺言
你信誓旦旦说爱我，可我看到什么
看到你过来泼我一身果汁
鸡零狗碎，鸡零狗碎
失去的时光找不回

现在，你拿来了账本按我低头
你说的一切我都不记得
你信誓旦旦说爱我，可我明白什么
你总是向我泼果汁，像是你有了地方去
鸡零狗碎，鸡零狗碎
失去的时光找不回

现在我受够了，清空了箱底
你知道我在说什么你也明白我意思
从现在起你最好找别人去
真这么做时，把那果汁留给你自己
鸡零狗碎，鸡零狗碎
失去的时光找不回

Odds and Ends

I plan it all and I take my place
You break your promise all over the place
You promised to love me, but what do I see
Just you comin' and spillin' juice over me
Odds and ends, odds and ends
Lost time is not found again

Now, you take your file and you bend my head
I never can remember anything that you said
You promised to love me, but what do I know
You're always spillin' juice on me like you got someplace to go
Odds and ends, odds and ends
Lost time is not found again

Now, I've had enough, my box is clean
You know what I'm sayin' and you know what I mean
From now on you'd best get on someone else
While you're doin' it, keep that juice to yourself
Odds and ends, odds and ends
Lost time is not found again

百万美元狂欢

哦，那傻大个金发女人
方向盘卡在乳沟间
"乌龟"，他们的朋友
支票全是假的
脸上堆满肉
钞票上沾着他的奶酪
他们全都将抵达
那百万美元狂欢
噢，宝贝，噢嘿
噢，宝贝，噢嘿
那可是百万美元狂欢

从现在开始每个人
都去那儿再回来
来时越喧哗的
垮得越厉害
来吧，甜奶油
别忘拍照
我们都会相会在
那百万美元狂欢

噢，宝贝，噢嘿

噢，宝贝，噢嘿

那可是百万美元狂欢

哦，我带了律师

去那仓房

蠢货内莉在那儿

她给他讲了个段子

然后琼斯来了

清空了垃圾

人人都前往

去那百万美元狂欢

噢，宝贝，噢嘿

噢，宝贝，噢嘿

那可是百万美元狂欢

哦，我撞得太狠

我的石头[1]都受不了

我早上起来了

但太早了，还没清醒

先是你好，再见

_____

1. 石头，俚语有"睾丸""胆量"之意。

然后推再然后撞

而我们都会及时到达

那百万美元狂欢

噢，宝贝，噢嘿

噢，宝贝，噢嘿

那可是百万美元狂欢

哦，我看着手表

看着我的手腕

往自己脸上

砸了一拳

我拿起马铃薯

拿去捣成泥

再转送到

那百万美元狂欢上

噢，宝贝，噢嘿

噢，宝贝，噢嘿

那可是百万美元狂欢

Million Dollar Bash

Well, that big dumb blonde
With her wheel in the gorge
And Turtle, that friend of theirs
With his checks all forged
And his cheeks in a chunk
With his cheese in the cash
They're all gonna be there
At that million dollar bash
Ooh, baby, ooh-ee
Ooh, baby, ooh-ee
It's that million dollar bash

Ev'rybody from right now
To over there and back
The louder they come
The harder they crack
Come now, sweet cream
Don't forget to flash
We're all gonna meet
At that million dollar bash
Ooh, baby, ooh-ee
Ooh, baby, ooh-ee
It's that million dollar bash

Well, I took my counselor
Out to the barn
Silly Nelly was there
She told him a yarn
Then along came Jones

Emptied the trash
Ev'rybody went down
To that million dollar bash
Ooh, baby, ooh-ee
Ooh, baby, ooh-ee
It's that million dollar bash

Well, I'm hittin' it too hard
My stones won't take
I get up in the mornin'
But it's too early to wake
First it's hello, goodbye
Then push and then crash
But we're all gonna make it
At that million dollar bash
Ooh, baby, ooh-ee
Ooh, baby, ooh-ee
It's that million dollar bash

Well, I looked at my watch
I looked at my wrist
Punched myself in the face
With my fist
I took my potatoes
Down to be mashed
Then I made it over
To that million dollar bash
Ooh, baby, ooh-ee
Ooh, baby, ooh-ee
It's that million dollar bash

去阿卡普尔科 [1]

我要去罗斯·玛丽那儿

她待我一直不错

她说话直来直去

唱支歌她就给我

生活很操蛋，但那又怎样

星星不会掉到地上

我站在泰姬陵外面

一个人影都没看见

去阿卡普尔科——继续在路上

去看看大肚腩——好好玩一场

呀——好好玩一场

现在，不管我何时起身

总是搞不懂我看到的

我就在三点一刻左右

去罗斯·玛丽那儿

———————————

1. 阿卡普尔科，墨西哥南部港口城市。

去那儿的路不好走

但是我一点儿也不抱怨

如果云彩不落雨而火车不停

我就注定会与太阳见面

去阿卡普尔科——继续在路上

去看看大肚腩——好好玩一场

呀——好好玩一场

现在，若有谁对我开玩笑

我都会说不用了谢谢

我尽可能实事求是地说

因此远离恶作剧

哦你知道，有时水井不出水

我就去压它那么几下

罗斯·玛丽，她喜欢去大地方

她会待在那儿，等着我到来

去阿卡普尔科——继续在路上

去看看大肚腩——好好玩一场

呀——好好玩一场

Goin' to Acapulco

I'm going down to Rose Marie's
She never does me wrong
She puts it to me plain as day
And gives it to me for a song

It's a wicked life but what the hell
The stars ain't falling down
I'm standing outside the Taj Mahal
I don't see no one around

Goin' to Acapulco—goin' on the run
Goin' down to see fat gut—goin' to have some fun
Yeah—goin' to have some fun

Now, whenever I get up
And I ain't got what I see
I just make it down to Rose Marie's
'Bout a quarter after three

There are worse ways of getting there
And I ain't complainin' none
If the clouds don't drop and the train don't stop
I'm bound to meet the sun

Goin' to Acapulco—goin' on the run
Goin' down to see fat gut—goin' to have some fun
Yeah—goin' to have some fun

Now, if someone offers me a joke

I just say no thanks
I try to tell it like it is
And keep away from pranks

Well, sometime you know when the well breaks down
I just go pump on it some
Rose Marie, she likes to go to big places
And just set there waitin' for me to come

Goin' to Acapulco—goin' on the run
Goin' down to see fat gut—goin' to have some fun
Yeah—goin' to have some fun

看哪!

我出发去圣安东
感觉从没这么好
我的女人说会在那儿和我见面
当然，我知道她会
那个赶车的拍我一下，把我从沉迷中叫醒
他问我的名字
我立即告诉了他
然后，我羞愧地垂着头
看哪！看哪！
寻找我的 "看哪"
我的好老弟，快带我离开这里！

我到了匹兹堡
刚好六点半
给自己找了个空位
然后，我摘下帽子
"怎么了，莫莉亲爱的
你的阴阜出了什么问题？"

"这和你有什么相干，莫比·迪克[1]?

这里是齐肯镇!"[2]

看哪! 看哪!

寻找我的"看哪"

我的好老弟，快带我离开这里!

我给我的女孩

买了一群麋鹿

一群属于她自己的麋鹿

哦，第二天她出来看

它们跑哪儿去了

我要去田纳西

找辆卡车什么的

攒点钱，再把它们都撕碎!

看哪! 看哪!

寻找我的"看哪"

我的好老弟，快带我离开这里!

现在，我坐着摩天轮进来了

---

1. 莫比·迪克，梅尔维尔同名小说中的鲸鱼名字，在俗语中引申为"大鸡巴"
之意。
2. 文字游戏，"这里是齐肯镇"双关"这里都是胆小鬼"。

孩子们，我肯定很油条

我像一吨砖头来了

对他们要上几个花招

我要回到匹兹堡

数到三十

绕过那远角，跨上鹿群

挽轭成列！

看哪！看哪！

寻找我的"看哪"

我的好老弟，快带我离开这里！

Lo and Behold!

I pulled out for San Anton'
I never felt so good
My woman said she'd meet me there
And of course, I knew she would
The coachman, he hit me for my hook
And he asked me my name
I give it to him right away
Then I hung my head in shame
Lo and behold! Lo and behold!
Lookin' for my lo and behold
Get me outa here, my dear man!

I come into Pittsburgh
At six-thirty flat
I found myself a vacant seat
An' I put down my hat
"What's the matter, Molly, dear
What's the matter with your mound?"
"What's it to ya, Moby Dick?
This is chicken town!"
Lo and behold! Lo and behold!
Lookin' for my lo and behold
Get me outa here, my dear man!

I bought my girl
A herd of moose
One she could call her own
Well, she came out the very next day
To see where they had flown

I'm goin' down to Tennessee
Get me a truck 'r somethin'
Gonna save my money and rip it up!
Lo and behold! Lo and behold!
Lookin' for my lo and behold
Get me outa here, my dear man!

Now, I come in on a Ferris wheel
An' boys, I sure was slick
I come in like a ton of bricks
Laid a few tricks on 'em
Goin' back to Pittsburgh
Count up to thirty
Round that horn and ride that herd
Gonna thread up!
Lo and behold! Lo and behold!
Lookin' for my lo and behold
Get me outa here, my dear man!

晾衣绳传奇

稍后我们把衣服改短

谁都没多说什么

只是几件皱的旧衬衣和两条裤子

没有人真的愿意碰

妈妈进来拿起一本书

爸爸问她是什么

其他人说："关你什么事？"

爸爸说："这个，不为什么"

然后他们开始取回他们的衣服

挂到绳子上

这是一月三十号

人人都感觉不错

第二天大家起来

看衣服干了没有

狗在叫，一个邻居经过

妈妈，当然她说："嗨！"

"你听说那新闻了吗？"他问，咧开嘴

"副总统疯了！"

"在哪？""城里。""什么时候？""昨晚"

"嗯，啧啧，这可真糟！"

"嗨，我们对此无能为力，"邻居说

"过不多久这事就会被忘掉"

"是的，我想也是。"妈妈说

然后她问我衣服是不是还湿着

我伸手，摸我的衬衣

邻居问："这些衣服是你的？"

我说："有些是，不全是"

他问："你总在帮忙干这些杂事？"

我说："有时候，不是所有时候"

然后邻居擤起了鼻涕

这时候爸爸在外面喊

"妈妈叫你把衣服给他们拿进屋"

哦，我只是听令行事

所以，我当然这样做了

我进了屋，妈妈迎着我

然后我关上所有的门

Clothes Line Saga

After a while we took in the clothes
Nobody said very much
Just some old wild shirts and a couple pairs of pants
Which nobody really wanted to touch
Mama come in and picked up a book
An' Papa asked her what it was
Someone else asked, "What do you care?"
Papa said, "Well, just because"
Then they started to take back their clothes
Hang 'em on the line
It was January the thirtieth
And everybody was feelin' fine

The next day everybody got up
Seein' if the clothes were dry
The dogs were barking, a neighbor passed
Mama, of course, she said, "Hi!"
"Have you heard the news?" he said, with a grin
"The Vice-President's gone mad!"
"Where?" "Downtown." "When?" "Last night"
"Hmm, say, that's too bad!"
"Well, there's nothin' we can do about it," said the neighbor
"It's just somethin' we're gonna have to forget"
"Yes, I guess so," said Ma
Then she asked me if the clothes was still wet

I reached up, touched my shirt
And the neighbor said, "Are those clothes yours?"
I said, "Some of 'em, not all of 'em"

He said, "Ya always help out around here with the chores?"
I said, "Sometime, not all the time"
Then my neighbor, he blew his nose
Just as Papa yelled outside
"Mama wants you t' come back in the house and bring
   them clothes"
Well, I just do what I'm told
So, I did it, of course
I went back in the house and Mama met me
And then I shut all the doors

小苹果树

老人划着小划子
去那儿
老人给鱼钩上了饵
在那儿
马上小小鱼钩要把人拖下去
马上要把人拖下小溪
噢，对！

这会儿，他在那棵小苹果树底下
噢，对！
在那棵小苹果树下
噢，对！
在那棵树底下
将只有你和我
在那棵小苹果树底下
噢，对！

我推他回去然后我排队等着
噢，对！
然后我让我的萨迪安静下来我排队等着

噢，对！

然后我让我的萨迪安静下来我排队等着

两眼一眨的工夫我上了船

噢，对！

在那棵小苹果树下

噢，对！

在那棵小苹果树下

噢，对！

在那棵树底下

就将会有你和我

在那棵小苹果树底下

噢，对！

这会儿，谁在桌子上，谁来告诉我？

噢，对！

谁在桌子上，谁来告诉我？

噢，对！

我应该告诉谁，啊，我应该告诉谁？

你们四十九个，像地狱里飞出的蝙蝠

啊在那棵古老的小苹果树底下

Apple Suckling Tree

Old man sailin' in a dinghy boat
Down there
Old man down is baitin' a hook
On there
Gonna pull man down on a suckling hook
Gonna pull man into the suckling brook
Oh yeah!

Now, he's underneath that apple suckling tree
Oh yeah!
Under that apple suckling tree
Oh yeah!
That's underneath that tree
There's gonna be just you and me
Underneath that apple suckling tree
Oh yeah!

I push him back and I stand in line
Oh yeah!
Then I hush my Sadie and stand in line
Oh yeah!
Then I hush my Sadie and stand in line
I get on board in two-eyed time
Oh yeah!

Under that apple suckling tree
Oh yeah!
Under that apple suckling tree
Oh yeah!

Underneath that tree
There's just gonna be you and me
Underneath that apple suckling tree
Oh yeah!

Now, who's on the table, who's to tell me?
Oh yeah!
Who's on the table, who's to tell me?
Oh yeah!
Who should I tell, oh, who should I tell?
The forty-nine of you like bats out of hell
Oh underneath that old apple suckling tree

求你啦，亨利太太

哦，我喝了两扎啤酒

准备好被扫出去

求你啦，亨利太太你能不能

把我领进我的屋？

我是个好小伙儿

但是我吃了太多蛋

跟太多人说话

灌了太多黄汤

求你啦，亨利太太，亨利太太，求求你！

求你啦，亨利太太，亨利太太，求求你！

我现在跪下啦

我一个子儿都没啦

哦，我在门厅呻吟着

再过不多会儿我要疯了

求你啦，亨利太太你能不能

带我去见你爹？

我能像鱼那样喝 [1]

———————

1. 像鱼那样喝，习语，意为牛饮。

像蛇那样爬

像火鸡那样咬

像鸭子那样啄

求你啦，亨利太太，亨利太太，求求你！

求你啦，亨利太太，亨利太太，求求你！

我现在跪下啦

我一个子儿都没啦

现在，别推我女士

不然我会灌你一鞋

我是亲爱的波旁¹老爹

今天晚上很忧郁

我已经一千岁了

是一颗慷慨的炸弹

生有丁字骨并穿了孔

但人们都知道我是个冷静的人

求你啦，亨利太太，亨利太太，求求你！

求你啦，亨利太太，亨利太太，求求你！

我现在跪下啦

我一个子儿都没啦

———————

1. 波旁，又指波本威士忌。

现在，我得去排排涝了

我的凳子就要吱吱嘎嘎响

要是我走太远

我的鹤儿就要出水

瞧，亨利太太

我能做的不过就是这些

为什么你不从我的角度看

再帮我满上几杯?

求你啦，亨利太太，亨利太太，求求你!

求你啦，亨利太太，亨利太太，求求你!

我现在跪下啦

我一个子儿都没啦

Please, Mrs. Henry

Well, I've already had two beers
I'm ready for the broom
Please, Missus Henry, won't you
Take me to my room?
I'm a good ol' boy
But I've been sniffin' too many eggs
Talkin' to too many people
Drinkin' too many kegs
Please, Missus Henry, Missus Henry, please!
Please, Missus Henry, Missus Henry, please!
I'm down on my knees
An' I ain't got a dime

Well, I'm groanin' in a hallway
Pretty soon I'll be mad
Please, Missus Henry, won't you
Take me to your dad?
I can drink like a fish
I can crawl like a snake
I can bite like a turkey
I can slam like a drake
Please, Missus Henry, Missus Henry, please!
Please, Missus Henry, Missus Henry, please!
I'm down on my knees
An' I ain't got a dime

Now, don't crowd me, lady
Or I'll fill up your shoe
I'm a sweet bourbon daddy

An' tonight I am blue
I'm a thousand years old
And I'm a generous bomb
I'm T-boned and punctured
But I'm known to be calm
Please, Missus Henry, Missus Henry, please!
Please, Missus Henry, Missus Henry, please!
I'm down on my knees
An' I ain't got a dime

Now, I'm startin' to drain
My stool's gonna squeak
If I walk too much farther
My crane's gonna leak
Look, Missus Henry
There's only so much I can do
Why don't you look my way
An' pump me a few?
Please, Missus Henry, Missus Henry, please!
Please, Missus Henry, Missus Henry, please!
I'm down on my knees
An' I ain't got a dime

愤怒的泪水

（与理查德·曼纽尔合作）

我们用我们的手臂抱着你

在独立日里

而现在你把我们扔一边儿

让我们自寻出路

噢天底下什么样的亲闺女

会这样对待她的父亲

无微不至地伺候他

又总是对他说"不"？

愤怒的泪水，悲伤的泪水

干吗我总得做个贼？

来我这儿吧，你知道的

我们如此孤单

而人生短暂

我们指给你要走的路

在沙地上画你的名字

你却觉得这不过是

让你有个立足之地而已

现在我要你明白，当我们照看着你

你发现无人出于真心

大多数人真正想的是

做这件事实在是幼稚

愤怒的泪水，悲伤的泪水

难道我总得做个贼吗？

来我这儿吧，你知道的

我们如此低贱

而人生短暂

这毫无痛苦

当你出去接受那些

我们永远不会信的

错误信条

而现在，心里装满了金子

仿佛它是一只钱包

但是，啊，这究竟是种什么爱

从坏变得更坏？

愤怒的泪水，悲伤的泪水

难道我总得做个贼吗？

来我这儿吧，你知道的

我们如此低贱

而人生短暂

Tears of Rage
(with Richard Manuel)

We carried you in our arms
On Independence Day
And now you'd throw us all aside
And put us on our way
Oh what dear daughter 'neath the sun
Would treat a father so
To wait upon him hand and foot
And always tell him, "No"?
Tears of rage, tears of grief
Why must I always be the thief?
Come to me now, you know
We're so alone
And life is brief

We pointed out the way to go
And scratched your name in sand
Though you just thought it was nothing more
Than a place for you to stand
Now, I want you to know that while we watched
You discover there was no one true
Most ev'rybody really thought
It was a childish thing to do
Tears of rage, tears of grief
Must I always be the thief?
Come to me now, you know
We're so low
And life is brief

It was all very painless
When you went out to receive
All that false instruction
Which we never could believe
And now the heart is filled with gold
As if it was a purse
But, oh, what kind of love is this
Which goes from bad to worse?
Tears of rage, tears of grief
Must I always be the thief?
Come to me now, you know
We're so low
And life is brief

太多虚无

现在，太多虚无

会让人感到不自在

可能一个人的脾气上来了

而另一个人的脾气结成了冰

忏悔的日子

我们不能嘲弄灵魂

啊，当有太多虚无

谁都无法控制

向瓦莱丽问好

向薇薇安 [1] 问好

给她们我所有的工钱

在遗忘泉边

太多虚无

会让人辱骂君王

他可以上街，像大多数人一样吹牛

但是他什么都不会明白

---

1. 瓦莱丽和薇薇安是 T. S. 艾略特两任妻子的名字。

哦，这一切都发生过
这一切都写入了一本书
可是，因为有太多虚无
没有人会去看

向瓦莱丽问好
向薇薇安问好
给她们我所有的工钱
在遗忘泉边

太多虚无
会让人变成骗子
会让一个人睡钉板
而另一个人吞食火焰
每个人都在做着什么
我在梦中听到了这些
可是，就因为有太多虚无
让小伙子变得刻薄

向瓦莱丽问好
向薇薇安问好
给她们我所有的工钱
在遗忘泉边

Too Much of Nothing

Now, too much of nothing
Can make a man feel ill at ease
One man's temper might rise
While another man's temper might freeze
In the day of confession
We cannot mock a soul
Oh, when there's too much of nothing
No one has control

Say hello to Valerie
Say hello to Vivian
Send them all my salary
On the waters of oblivion

Too much of nothing
Can make a man abuse a king
He can walk the streets and boast like most
But he wouldn't know a thing
Now, it's all been done before
It's all been written in the book
But when there's too much of nothing
Nobody should look

Say hello to Valerie
Say hello to Vivian
Send them all my salary
On the waters of oblivion

Too much of nothing

Can turn a man into a liar
It can cause one man to sleep on nails
And another man to eat fire
Ev'rybody's doin' somethin'
I heard it in a dream
But when there's too much of nothing
It just makes a fella mean

Say hello to Valerie
Say hello to Vivian
Send them all my salary
On the waters of oblivion

是啊！很重而且还有一瓶面包

哦，小人书和我，就我们俩，赶上了公共汽车
但可怜的小司机，她回床去睡觉
第二天，鼻子里满是浓鼻涕
是啊！很重而且还有一瓶面包
是啊！很重而且还有一瓶面包
是啊！很重而且还有一瓶面包

这是一条道的城，只有棕色，还有微风
包起肉，宝贝儿，我们要出门
向一堆水果中的威奇托进发
去夺战利品，动作快点，我们去弄条鳟鱼
去夺战利品，动作快点，我们去弄条鳟鱼
去夺战利品，动作快点，我们去弄条鳟鱼

现在，把那鼓手从那瓶子后面拖出来
把我的烟斗带给我，我们要去摇一摇
用变了味儿的派拍那鼓手
带我去加利福尼亚，亲爱的
带我去加利福尼亚，亲爱的
带我去加利福尼亚，亲爱的

是的，小人书和我，就我们俩，赶上了公共汽车

但可怜的小司机，她回床去睡觉

第二天，鼻子里满是浓鼻涕

是啊！很重而且还有一瓶面包

是啊！很重而且还有一瓶面包

是啊！很重而且还有一瓶面包

Yea! Heavy and a Bottle of Bread

Well, the comic book and me, just us, we caught the bus
The poor little chauffeur, though, she was back in bed
On the very next day, with a nose full of pus
Yea! Heavy and a bottle of bread
Yea! Heavy and a bottle of bread
Yea! Heavy and a bottle of bread

It's a one-track town, just brown, and a breeze, too
Pack up the meat, sweet, we're headin' out
For Wichita in a pile of fruit
Get the loot, don't be slow, we're gonna catch a trout
Get the loot, don't be slow, we're gonna catch a trout
Get the loot, don't be slow, we're gonna catch a trout

Now, pull that drummer out from behind that bottle
Bring me my pipe, we're gonna shake it
Slap that drummer with a pie that smells
Take me down to California, baby
Take me down to California, baby
Take me down to California, baby

Yes, the comic book and me, just us, we caught the bus
The poor little chauffeur, though, she was back in bed
On the very next day, with a nose full of pus
Yea! Heavy and a bottle of bread
Yea! Heavy and a bottle of bread
Yea! Heavy and a bottle of bread

坠入洪流

大堤决口了，妈妈

洪水就要泛滥

沼泽将会扩大

将没有船能够划行

现在，你可以乘火车

去威廉斯角

你可以踏破脚

可以摇晃关节

可是啊妈妈，这时你不想念你最好的朋友吗？

最好的朋友

你得为自己另找一个，无论如何

现在，别想打动我

你就快要失败

大堤破了道口子

而妈妈，你已经被拒绝

喏，这就是以糖还糖

以盐还盐

如果你坠入洪流

这将是你自己的错

啊妈妈，这时你不想念你最好的朋友吗？

最好的朋友

你得为自己另找一个，无论如何

哦，潮水正上涨

妈妈，请不要叫我失望

去收拾行李吧

妈妈，不要弄出声响

喏，这就是以王还王

以后还后

这会是一场，所有人见过的

最无情的洪水

啊妈妈，这时你不想念你最好的朋友吗？

是的，最好的朋友

你得为自己另找一个，无论如何

Down in the Flood

Crash on the levee, mama
Water's gonna overflow
Swamp's gonna rise
No boat's gonna row
Now, you can train on down
To Williams Point
You can bust your feet
You can rock this joint
But oh mama, ain't you gonna miss your best friend now?
You're gonna have to find yourself
Another best friend, somehow

Now, don't you try an' move me
You're just gonna lose
There's a crash on the levee
And, mama, you've been refused
Well, it's sugar for sugar
And salt for salt
If you go down in the flood
It's gonna be your own fault
Oh mama, ain't you gonna miss your best friend now?
You're gonna have to find yourself
Another best friend, somehow

Well, that high tide's risin'
Mama, don't you let me down
Pack up your suitcase
Mama, don't you make a sound
Now, it's king for king

Queen for queen
It's gonna be the meanest flood
That anybody's seen
Oh mama, ain't you gonna miss your best friend now?
Yes, you're gonna have to find yourself
Another best friend, somehow

小蒙哥马利

哦你可以告诉大家
在老旧金山
告诉他们
小蒙哥马利前来问候

马上每个男孩女孩
都会得到大惊喜
因为小蒙哥马利
就要摇起那玩意儿
去告诉大家
在老旧金山
小蒙哥马利来了
来说问候

"瘦哞哞"和
"半履带车"弗兰克
他们俩都会
爬出舱来
独鸟书
和秃鹰和乌鸦

告诉他们各位

小蒙要来问候

挠你爹

做那鸟

舔那猪

然后带它回家

捡起水滴

然后烤那面团

告诉他们各位

小蒙前来问候

现在他是醉汉之王

并且他也在挤

当心了李斯特

拿着，卢

加入僧侣队伍

产联[1]

告诉他们各位

小蒙哥马利前来问候

---

1. 即美国产业工人联合会，成立于 1905 年，1955 年与美国劳动联合会合并。

现在给猪抹油

并且唱赞歌

跑出去

给那只狗加气

捉弄捉弄

按出臭气

放下来

然后看着它长

放低

再抬高

把它装进

采集杯

三腿人

和烈唇锄

告诉他们各位

蒙哥马利前来问候

哦你可以告诉大家

在老旧金山

告诉他们各位

蒙哥马利前来问候

Tiny Montgomery

Well you can tell ev'rybody
Down in ol' Frisco
Tell 'em
Tiny Montgomery says hello

Now ev'ry boy and girl's
Gonna get their bang
'Cause Tiny Montgomery's
Gonna shake that thing
Tell ev'rybody
Down in ol' Frisco
That Tiny Montgomery's comin'
Down to say hello

Skinny Moo and
Half-track Frank
They're gonna both be gettin'
Outa the tank
One bird book
And a buzzard and a crow
Tell 'em all
That Tiny's gonna say hello

Scratch your dad
Do that bird
Suck that pig
And bring it on home
Pick that drip
And bake that dough

Tell 'em all
That Tiny says hello

Now he's king of the drunks
An' he squeezes, too
Watch out, Lester
Take it, Lou
Join the monks
The C.I.O.
Tell 'em all
That Tiny Montgomery says hello

Now grease that pig
And sing praise
Go on out
And gas that dog
Trick on in
Honk that stink
Take it on down
And watch it grow
Play it low
And pick it up
Take it on in
In a plucking cup
Three-legged man
And a hot-lipped hoe
Tell 'em all
Montgomery says hello

Well you can tell ev'rybody
Down in ol' Frisco
Tell 'em all
Montgomery says hello

哪儿也不去

云朵飞动

雨不会消

门不会关

栅栏冻住

将心神远离冬天

哪儿也不去

呜喂！带我到高处吧

明天就是大日子

我的新娘会来到

噢，噢，我们会飞吗

就在这安乐椅上！

我才不管

他们发了多少信

早晨降临了又过去

拿好钱

收拾好帐篷

哪儿也不去

呜喂！带我到高处吧

明天就是大日子

我的新娘会来到

噢，噢，我们会飞吗

就在这安乐椅上！

给我买支长笛

和一支能射的枪

车后盖和代用品

捆起自己

在那扎着根的树上

哪儿也不去

呜喂！带我到高处吧

明天就是大日子

我的新娘会来到

噢，噢，我们会飞吗

就在这安乐椅上！

成吉思汗

保不住他的

所有的王

补充好睡眠

我们将爬上那山岗，不管多陡

当我们爬上去

呜喂！带我到高处吧

明天就是大日子

我的新娘会来到

噢，噢，我们会飞吗

就在这安乐椅上！

You Ain't Goin' Nowhere

Clouds so swift
Rain won't lift
Gate won't close
Railings froze
Get your mind off wintertime
You ain't goin' nowhere
Whoo-ee! Ride me high
Tomorrow's the day
My bride's gonna come
Oh, oh, are we gonna fly
Down in the easy chair!

I don't care
How many letters they sent
Morning came and morning went
Pick up your money
And pack up your tent
You ain't goin' nowhere
Whoo-ee! Ride me high
Tomorrow's the day
My bride's gonna come
Oh, oh, are we gonna fly
Down in the easy chair!

Buy me a flute
And a gun that shoots
Tailgates and substitutes
Strap yourself
To the tree with roots

You ain't goin' nowhere
Whoo-ee! Ride me high
Tomorrow's the day
My bride's gonna come
Oh, oh, are we gonna fly
Down in the easy chair!

Genghis Khan
He could not keep
All his kings
Supplied with sleep
We'll climb that hill no matter how steep
When we get up to it
Whoo-ee! Ride me high
Tomorrow's the day
My bride's gonna come
Oh, oh, are we gonna fly
Down in the easy chair!

不要告诉亨利

不要告诉亨利
苹果上落了你的苍蝇

星期六清早，我去河边
环顾下四周，看看有没有人出现
就看见一个胆小鬼在那儿跪着
我走过去冲他喊："起来，起来，起来！"
他说："不要告诉亨利
不要告诉亨利
不要告诉亨利
说苹果上落了你的苍蝇"

十点半，我去街拐角
我四处张望，不敢说何时
我往下看看，我往上看
而我看见的人，只有我爱的那位
她说："不要告诉亨利
不要告诉亨利
不要告诉亨利
说苹果上落了你的苍蝇"

然后，十二点半，我去小餐馆

环顾四周，只看见我自己

也认出一匹马和一头驴

我想找头牛，还真看到了几头

它们说："不要告诉亨利

不要告诉亨利

不要告诉亨利

说苹果上落了你的苍蝇"

然后，前两天的夜里，我去了泵房

环顾四周，可它却不见了

我上下望着，找那棵高大的老树

我确实上了楼，但除了我，我没看见人

我说："不要告诉亨利

不要告诉亨利

不要告诉亨利

说苹果上落了你的苍蝇"

Don't Ya Tell Henry

Don't ya tell Henry
Apple's got your fly

I went down to the river on a Saturday morn
A-lookin' around just to see who's born
I found a little chicken down on his knees
I went up and yelled to him, "Please, please, please!"
He said, "Don't ya tell Henry
Don't ya tell Henry
Don't ya tell Henry
Apple's got your fly"

I went down to the corner at a-half past ten
I's lookin' around, I wouldn't say when
I looked down low, I looked above
And who did I see but the one I love
She said, "Don't ya tell Henry
Don't ya tell Henry
Don't ya tell Henry
Apple's got your fly"

Now, I went down to the beanery at half past twelve
A-lookin' around just to see myself
I spotted a horse and a donkey, too
I looked for a cow and I saw me a few
They said, "Don't ya tell Henry
Don't ya tell Henry
Don't ya tell Henry
Apple's got your fly"

Now, I went down to the pumphouse the other night
A-lookin' around, it was outa sight
I looked high and low for that big ol' tree
I did go upstairs but I didn't see nobody but me
I said, "Don't ya tell Henry
Don't ya tell Henry
Don't ya tell Henry
Apple's got your fly"

什么都未交付

什么都未交付

而且，我告诉你这一事实

不是出于怨恨或愤怒

就只因为它是事实

现在，我希望你对此不会反对

把你欠的都还回来

你越少废话

就可以越早离开

没有更好，没有最好

你给我听好了，然后好好歇歇

什么都未交付

可我不能说我同情

你即将到来的命运

是的，为了你撒的所有那些谎

现在你必须，为你卖了却没到的货

提供一些解决办法

你越早提出来

就可以越早离开

没有更好，没有最好

你给我听好了，然后好好歇歇

（如今你知道了）

什么都未交付

那么，随你爱说不说

你让每个人付钱时

你心里究竟在想什么

不，什么都未交付

是的，必须有人做出解释

就只需要这样

然后你就可以滚蛋

没有更好，没有最好

你给我听好了，然后好好歇歇

Nothing Was Delivered

Nothing was delivered
And I tell this truth to you
Not out of spite or anger
But simply because it's true
Now, I hope you won't object to this
Giving back all of what you owe
The fewer words you have to waste on this
The sooner you can go

Nothing is better, nothing is best
Take heed of this and get plenty of rest

Nothing was delivered
But I can't say I sympathize
With what your fate is going to be
Yes, for telling all those lies
Now you must provide some answers
For what you sell has not been received
And the sooner you come up with them
The sooner you can leave

Nothing is better, nothing is best
Take heed of this and get plenty rest

(Now you know)
Nothing was delivered
And it's up to you to say
Just what you had in mind
When you made ev'rybody pay

No, nothing was delivered
Yes, 'n' someone must explain
That as long as it takes to do this
Then that's how long that you'll remain

Nothing is better, nothing is best
Take heed of this and get plenty rest

开门，荷马 [1]

哎，有这么件事

我从吉姆那儿知道的

他一直在确认我听懂了

他说一个人必须

以某种方式游

如果他指望过上

地肥物美的生活

开门，荷马

这事情我听过

开门，荷马

这事情我听过

但我不想再听了

现在，有这么件事

我从我朋友"老鼠"那儿知道的

一个总是红脸的伙计

他说每个人

---

1. "荷马"是迪伦的朋友理查德·法里纳（Richard Fariña）的绰号。法里纳在 1966 年 4 月死于摩托车事故，同年 7 月迪伦也在摩托车事故中受伤。

都得把自己的房子冲干净

如果他不想

到处去清洗房子

开门，荷马

这事情我听过

开门，荷马

这事情我听过

但我不想再听了

"照看好你所有的记忆"

我的朋友米克说

"因为你不可能重新经历

并且要记住，当你到了那儿

试图救治病人

你永远必须

先原谅他们"

开门，荷马

这事情我听过

开门，荷马

这事情我听过

但我不想再听了

Open the Door, Homer

Now, there's a certain thing
That I learned from Jim
That he'd always make sure I'd understand
And that is that there's a certain way
That a man must swim
If he expects to live off
Of the fat of the land
Open the door, Homer
I've heard it said before
Open the door, Homer
I've heard it said before
But I ain't gonna hear it said no more

Now, there's a certain thing
That I learned from my friend, Mouse
A fella who always blushes
And that is that ev'ryone
Must always flush out his house
If he don't expect to be
Goin' 'round housing flushes
Open the door, Homer
I've heard it said before
Open the door, Homer
I've heard it said before
But I ain't gonna hear it said no more

"Take care of all your memories"
Said my friend, Mick
"For you cannot relive them

And remember when you're out there
Tryin' to heal the sick
That you must always
First forgive them"
Open the door, Homer
I've heard it said before
Open the door, Homer
I've heard it said before
But I ain't gonna hear it said no more

长途接线员

长途接线员
接通这电话，这可不是闹着玩儿
长途接线员
求你接通这电话，你知道这可不是闹着玩儿
我有个消息要给我宝贝儿
你知道，她可不是一般人

电话亭有数千人
数千人在门口
电话亭有数千人
数千人在门口
每个人都想打个长途电话
但是你知道他们只能再等等

如果从路易斯安那来了电话
求你，让它通过
如果从路易斯安那来了电话
求你，让它通过
这个电话亭要着火了
里面越来越热

人人都想做我朋友

但是没人想飞得更高

人人都想做我朋友

但是没人想飞得更高

长途接线员

我相信我就要勒死在这电话线上

Long-Distance Operator

Long-distance operator
Place this call, it's not for fun
Long-distance operator
Please, place this call, you know it's not for fun
I gotta get a message to my baby
You know, she's not just anyone

There are thousands in the phone booth
Thousands at the gate
There are thousands in the phone booth
Thousands at the gate
Ev'rybody wants to make a long-distance call
But you know they're just gonna have to wait

If a call comes from Louisiana
Please, let it ride
If a call comes from Louisiana
Please, let it ride
This phone booth's on fire
It's getting hot inside

Ev'rybody wants to be my friend
But nobody wants to get higher
Ev'rybody wants to be my friend
But nobody wants to get higher
Long-distance operator
I believe I'm stranglin' on this telephone wire

这车轮烧起来了

（与里克·丹科合作）

如果你的记性够好

那么我们应该会再相见并等待

所以我要打开行李取出所有东西

然后坐下来，以免为时已迟

这世上的人没谁会来找你

讲述另一个传说

但是你知道我们将再相见

如果你的记性够好

这车轮烧起来了

沿道路滚动着

最好去通知我的亲人

这车轮就要爆炸！

如果你的记性够好

我要没收掉你的饰带

用水手结包好

藏在你的匣子里

假若我确切地知道它属于你……

但是啊这很难说

但是你曾知道我们会再相见

如果你的记性够好

这车轮烧起来了

沿道路滚动着

最好去通知我的亲人

这车轮就要爆炸！

如果你的记性够好

那么你会记得，正是你

让我去找他们

帮你的忙

在每一个计划都失败之后

再没有什么更多的可说

你曾知道我们会再相见

如果你的记性够好

这车轮烧起来了

沿道路滚动着

最好去通知我的亲人

这车轮就要爆炸！

This Wheel's on Fire

(with Rick Danko)

If your mem'ry serves you well
We were goin' to meet again and wait
So I'm goin' to unpack all my things
And sit before it gets too late
No man alive will come to you
With another tale to tell
But you know that we shall meet again
If your mem'ry serves you well
This wheel's on fire
Rolling down the road
Best notify my next of kin
This wheel shall explode!

If your mem'ry serves you well
I was goin' to confiscate your lace
And wrap it up in a sailor's knot
And hide it in your case
If I knew for sure that it was yours...
But it was oh so hard to tell
But you knew that we would meet again
If your mem'ry serves you well
This wheel's on fire
Rolling down the road
Best notify my next of kin
This wheel shall explode!

If your mem'ry serves you well

You'll remember you're the one
That called on me to call on them
To get you your favors done
And after ev'ry plan had failed
And there was nothing more to tell
You knew that we would meet again
If your mem'ry served you well
This wheel's on fire
Rolling down the road
Best notify my next of kin
This wheel shall explode!

十字架上的名号 [1]

哦，我努力，啊这么久了

我只是努力地活着

那么现在，噢这是座金矿

可是这样真不错

是的，但是我的脑海里知道

我们全都被误导了

是十字架上的那个古老名号

令我烦忧

话说，当我还是个哭闹孩子的时候

我知道了我要成为哪种人

而这全都是因为

我应该看见的那个图像

但是我迷失在月球上

此时我听见前门呼地关上

十字架上的那个古老名号

1.《新约·约翰福音》19:19："彼拉多又用牌子写了一个名号，安在十字架上，写的是：'犹太人的王，拿撒勒人耶稣。'"注释凡涉《圣经》处，译文一律引自和合本，供大致的参照；《圣经》中屡见者，一般仅引一条。

依然令我烦忧

哦，是十字架上的那个古老名号
哦，是开启王国的那把古老钥匙
哦，是十字架上的那个古老名号
像是从前的你
但是，当我把头抬这么高
看到我的老友一个个走过
依然是十字架上的那个名号
令我烦忧

是的，那看起来就是十字架上的那个名号。每一天，每一夜，看见十字架上的名号，就矗立在山顶。是的，我们以为它可能早就消失了，但是在这里，我告诉你，朋友，恐怕它还在那儿立着呢。是的，你可能说，你只需要一些时间，但我不再那么确定了，因为那只鸟在这里，而你或许想进入其中，不过，当然，门也许关着。然而，我只想告诉你一次，假如我不会再见到你，我要说的是：十字架上的那个名号，是你可能最需要的东西。

是的，十字架上的名号
只不过是十字架上的一个名号
哦，每一把凿子上都有

而且那锦标里也有

啊，当你的，当你的日子屈指可数

而黑夜漫长

你也许会认识到你很软弱

但我的意思是你很刚强 [1]

是的你很刚强，假如十字架上的那个名号

假如它开始令你烦忧

哦，这都没什么，因为唱首歌

你的所有烦恼就都将过去

1.《新约·哥林多后书》12∶10∶"因我什么时候软弱，什么时候就刚强了。"

Sign on the Cross

Now, I try, oh for so awf'ly long
And I just try to be
And now, oh it's a gold mine
But it's so fine
Yes, but I know in my head
That we're all so misled
And it's that ol' sign on the cross
That worries me

Now, when I was just a bawlin' child
I saw what I wanted to be
And it's all for the sake
Of that picture I should see
But I was lost on the moon
As I heard that front door slam
And that old sign on the cross
Still worries me

Well, it's that old sign on the cross
Well, it's that old key to the kingdom
Well, it's that old sign on the cross
Like you used to be
But, when I hold my head so high
As I see my ol' friends go by
And it's still that sign on the cross
That worries me

Well, it seem to be the sign on the cross. Ev'ry day,
ev'ry night, see the sign on the cross just layin' up

on top of the hill. Yes, we thought it might have
disappeared long ago, but I'm here to tell you, friends,
that I'm afraid it's lyin' there still. Yes, just a
little time is all you need, you might say, but I don't
know 'bout that any more, because the bird is here and
you might want to enter it, but, of course, the door might
be closed. But I just would like to tell you one time,
if I don't see you again, that the thing is, that the sign
on the cross is the thing you might need the most.

Yes, the sign on the cross
Is just a sign on the cross
Well, there is some on every chisel
And there is some in the championship, too
Oh, when your, when your days are numbered
And your nights are long
You might think you're weak
But I mean to say you're strong
Yes you are, if that sign on the cross
If it begins to worry you
Well, that's all right because sing a song
And all your troubles will pass right on through

爱斯基摩人魁恩 [1]
（威猛魁恩）

每个人都在建大船小艇

也有的在建纪念碑

其他的，匆匆记下笔记

每个人都很绝望

每个女孩和男孩

但是等爱斯基摩人魁恩一到

每个人都会高兴得蹦起来

外面的都来吧，里面的都来吧

你不会再见到像威猛魁恩这样的人物

我喜欢像其他人一样做，我喜欢我的糖很甜

但是守着烟气或者仓皇奔走

都不是我的菜

每一个人都在树阴下

喂那树枝上的鸽子

但是等爱斯基摩人魁恩一到

---

1. 可能指涉美国演员安东尼·奎恩（Anthony Quinn）在电影《雪海冰上人》（*The Savage Innocents*，1960）中扮演的爱斯基摩人一角。

所有的鸽子都将奔向他

外面的都来吧，里面的都来吧

你不会再见到像威猛魁恩这样的人物

猫的喵喵和牛的哞哞，我都能背诵

只要告诉我你哪里疼，亲爱的

我就会告诉你该喊谁来

所有的人都睡不着

每个人的脚趾都被人踩着

但是等爱斯基摩人魁恩一到

每个人都要打起瞌睡

外面的都来吧，里面的都来吧

你不会再见到像威猛魁恩这样的人物

Quinn the Eskimo
(The Mighty Quinn)

Ev'rybody's building the big ships and the boats
Some are building monuments
Others, jotting down notes
Ev'rybody's in despair
Ev'ry girl and boy
But when Quinn the Eskimo gets here
Ev'rybody's gonna jump for joy
Come all without, come all within
You'll not see nothing like the mighty Quinn

I like to do just like the rest, I like my sugar sweet
But guarding fumes and making haste
It ain't my cup of meat
Ev'rybody's 'neath the trees
Feeding pigeons on a limb
But when Quinn the Eskimo gets here
All the pigeons gonna run to him
Come all without, come all within
You'll not see nothing like the mighty Quinn

A cat's meow and a cow's moo, I can recite 'em all
Just tell me where it hurts yuh, honey
And I'll tell you who to call
Nobody can get no sleep
There's someone on ev'ryone's toes
But when Quinn the Eskimo gets here
Ev'rybody's gonna wanna doze

Come all without, come all within
You'll not see nothing like the mighty Quinn

我将获得自由

他们说任何东西皆可替代
然而所有的距离都不近
因此我记住了，把我丢到这里来的
每个人的脸
我看见我的灯亮起来
从西直到东
不定哪天，不定哪天
我将获得自由

他们说每个人都需要保护
他们说每个人都有跌倒的时候
然而我发誓我看见了自己的样子
在远远高于这墙的某处
我看见我的灯亮起来
从西直到东
不定哪天，不定哪天
我将获得自由

在这孤独的人群中，站我旁边的
是一个发誓他不该受责罚的人

终日我听他大声叫喊

叫喊说他是被陷害的

我看见我的灯亮起来

从西直到东

不定哪天，不定哪天

我将获得自由

I Shall Be Released

They say ev'rything can be replaced
Yet ev'ry distance is not near
So I remember ev'ry face
Of ev'ry man who put me here
I see my light come shining
From the west unto the east
Any day now, any day now
I shall be released

They say ev'ry man needs protection
They say ev'ry man must fall
Yet I swear I see my reflection
Some place so high above this wall
I see my light come shining
From the west unto the east
Any day now, any day now
I shall be released

Standing next to me in this lonely crowd
Is a man who swears he's not to blame
All day long I hear him shout so loud
Crying out that he was framed
I see my light come shining
From the west unto the east
Any day now, any day now
I shall be released

把你的石头拿开！

你知道，有两个老女仆躺在床上

一个爬起来而另一个，她说：

"把你的石头拿开！

把你的石头拿开！（拿开！）

把你的石头拿开！（拿开！）

把你的石头从我身上拿开！（拿开！）"

哦，你知道，有一天深夜在蓝莓山

一个人转向另一个人说，以冻结血液的寒冷，他说：

"把你的石头拿开！（拿开！）

把你的石头拿开！（拿开！）

把你的石头拿开！（拿开！）

把你的石头从我身上拿开！（拿开！）"

哦，你知道，我们在貂肉溪畔躺着

一个人对另一个人说，他开口了，他说：

"把你的石头拿开！（拿开！）

把你的石头拿开！（拿开！）

把你的石头拿开！（拿开！）

把你的石头从我身上拿开！（拿开！）"

哦，你知道，我们坐着灰狗巴士在高速公路驰行

各种孩子在路边，冲我们叫嚷，说：

"把你们的石头拿开！（拿开！）

把你们的石头拿开！（拿开！）

把你们的石头拿开！（拿开！）

把你们的石头从我身上拿开！"

Get Your Rocks Off!

You know, there's two ol' maids layin' in the bed
One picked herself up an' the other one, she said:
"Get your rocks off!
Get your rocks off! (Get 'em off!)
Get your rocks off! (Get 'em off!)
Get your rocks off-a me! (Get 'em off!)"

Well, you know, there late one night up on Blueberry Hill
One man turned to the other man and said, with a blood-
    curdlin' chill, he said:
"Get your rocks off! (Get 'em off!)
Get your rocks off! (Get 'em off!)
Get your rocks off! (Get 'em off!)
Get your rocks off-a me! (Get 'em off!)"

Well, you know, we was layin' down around Mink Muscle
    Creek
One man said to the other man, he began to speak, he said:
"Get your rocks off! (Get 'em off!)
Get your rocks off! (Get 'em off!)
Get your rocks off! (Get 'em off!)
Get your rocks off-a me! (Get 'em off!)"

Well, you know, we was cruisin' down the highway in a
    Greyhound bus
All kinds-a children in the side road, they was hollerin' at
    us, sayin':
"Get your rocks off! (Get 'em off!)
Get your rocks off! (Get 'em off!)

Get your rocks off! (Get 'em off!)
Get your rocks off-a me!"

不说话的周末

不说话的周末

我的宝贝给了我

不说话的周末

我的宝贝给了我

她态度强硬

说这不是我的派对

她丢下了我在痛苦中

不说话的周末

我的宝贝让我吃一惊

不说话的周末

我的宝贝让我吃一惊

她摇摆又旋转

头冲着天花板

和别的男人一起晃着

不说话的周末

主啊，我希望星期一到来

不说话的周末

主啊，我当然希望星期一到来

她傲慢，她转圈
她乐颠颠，她溜达漫步
到自动点唱机边，装聋作哑

嗯，对这许许多多欺骗我想了许许多多
而我，也许我犯下的一些只是为了愉悦
但是在我们讲和后我捶打了许多披萨
这让你屈膝跪地

不说话的周末
我还活着，脑子快烧完了
不说话的周末
我还活着，脑子快烧完了
她知道我什么时候是闹着玩
而这大概不是
打开旅客列车门的时节

Silent Weekend

Silent weekend
My baby she gave it to me
Silent weekend
My baby she gave it to me
She's actin' tough and hardy
She says it ain't my party
And she's leavin' me in misery

Silent weekend
My baby she took me by surprise
Silent weekend
My baby she took me by surprise
She's rockin' and a-reelin'
Head up to ceiling
An' swinging with some other guys

Silent weekend
Oh Lord, I wish Monday would come
Silent weekend
Oh Lord, I sure wish Monday would come
She's uppity, she's rollin'
She's in the groove, she's strolling
Over to the jukebox playin' deaf and dumb

Well, I done a whole lotta thinkin' 'bout a whole lot of cheatin'
And I, maybe I did some just to please
But I just walloped a lotta pizza after makin' our peace
Puts ya down on bended knees

Silent weekend
Man alive, I'm burnin' up on my brain
Silent weekend
Man alive, I'm burnin' up on my brain
She knows when I'm just teasin'
But it's not likely in the season
To open up a passenger train

圣达菲

圣达菲，亲爱、亲爱、亲爱、亲爱、亲爱的圣达菲
我的女人每天都需要它
她答应这小伙儿她会留下
她卷起很多面包扔掉

她在圣达菲，亲爱、亲爱、亲爱、亲爱、亲爱的圣达菲
这会儿她打开了老处女的家门
她很骄傲，但是她需要漂泊
她会给自己写一首关于圣达菲的路边诗

圣达菲，亲爱、亲爱、亲爱、亲爱、亲爱的圣达菲
既然我永远不会停止漂泊
那么我从来就不会远离家
但我会造一座网格球顶，然后远航

不要难过，不、不、不、不、不要难过
这是我吃过的最好的食物
我特别高兴的是
她用自制的隔热垫做饭
我不在的时候她从未得过这么重的感冒

圣达菲，亲爱、亲爱、亲爱、亲爱、亲爱、亲爱的圣达菲
我的捕虾船在海湾
我不想我的本性变成这样
每一天我都倚靠在轮舵上，让船漂离

圣达菲，亲爱、亲爱、亲爱、亲爱、亲爱的圣达菲
我妹妹在家看来不错
她舔着冰淇淋蛋筒
收起她的大白梳子
它重量是多少？

Santa Fe

Santa Fe, dear, dear, dear, dear, dear Santa Fe
My woman needs it ev'ryday
She promised this a-lad she'd stay
She's rollin' up a lotta bread to toss away

She's in Santa Fe, dear, dear, dear, dear, dear Santa Fe
Now she's opened up an old maid's home
She's proud, but she needs to roam
She's gonna write herself a roadside poem about Santa Fe

Santa Fe, dear, dear, dear, dear, dear Santa Fe
Since I'm never gonna cease to roam
I'm never, ever far from home
But I'll build a geodesic dome and sail away

Don't feel bad, no, no, no, no, don't feel bad
It's the best food I've ever had
Makes me feel so glad
That she's cooking in a homemade pad
She never caught a cold so bad when I'm away

Santa Fe, dear, dear, dear, dear, dear Santa Fe
My shrimp boat's in the bay
I won't have my nature this way
And I'm leanin' on the wheel each day to drift away from

Santa Fe, dear, dear, dear, dear, dear Santa Fe
My sister looks good at home
She's lickin' on an ice cream cone

She's packin' her big white comb
What does it weigh?

Bob Dylan

PA
GAR
& B
THE

RETT
ILLY
KID

① Climbed upon the bell tower to gaze around at the terrain
I couldn't find you anywhere, you were gone like
a northern train

帕特·加勒特与比利小子
Pat Garrett & Billy the Kid

西川 译

　　《帕特·加勒特与比利小子》发行于 1973 年 7 月 13 日，是同名电影的原声专辑。该片编剧鲁迪·沃利策（Rudy Wurlitzer）及饰演比利小子的克里斯·克里斯托弗森（Kris Kristofferson），皆是迪伦的好友，后者还是一名民谣歌手。在这两位朋友的支持下，迪伦不仅成为了电影配乐的制作者，更出演了片中的一个角色。

　　事实上，导演萨姆·佩金帕（Sam Peckinpah）本身属意乡村歌手罗杰·米勒（Roger Miller），作为导演配乐老搭档的杰瑞·菲尔丁（Jerry Fielding）也不信任迪伦，质疑其能否胜任整部电影的音乐编排，起初更拒绝了迪伦所写的一首歌。但迪伦的创作最终还是获得了成功，当中包括日后广为人知的《敲着天堂的大门》。

　　《敲着天堂的大门》原本只是描述影片中的帕特·加勒特靠出卖朋友比利当上了警长，而比利自愿死于枪下，没有反抗，歌词将帕特的懊悔之情描摹得十分到位。在后来的流传和翻唱中，这首歌渐被赋予了反战的意涵。

从整体上看，这张专辑与其说刻画出了西部世界的粗犷，不如说令比利的传奇在苍凉中多了一丝温暖和亲切。层层递进的打击乐与原声乐器、电子乐器的编排，烘托出非常独特的冥思氛围，有一种凯鲁亚克式的禅宗意境。与迪伦的其他专辑比起来，这张西部片配乐反而可说是相当平和的作品。

编者

比利 [1]

河那边的枪口瞄着你
追踪你的执法者要逮着你
为领赏猎人们也想抓住你
比利，他们不愿你来去自由

整夜露宿在"百伦达" [2] 上
在庄园里打牌直到见天光
他们要扔你到靴子岗 [3] 上
比利，你是否不再搭理我

泡上个小妞 [4] 甜甜蜜蜜
她将带你穿过她的走廊幽寂
她将在孤独的阴影中迎向你
比利，你离家已经太远

---

1. 比利小子（Billy the Kid，1859—1881）为美国西部著名枪手，后被警长帕特·加勒特（Pat Garrett，1850—1908）击杀。
2. "百伦达"，马来语解作"针织物"。而在《比利》其他版本作"游廊"（veranda）。
3. 靴子岗，美国西部的牛仔但凡死于枪战或绞刑，当时有形容为"穿着靴子死"（die with one's boots on），故埋葬的坟茔俗称"靴子岗"。
4. 原文为西班牙语。

有人监视在镜后在空旷之地

在两屋之间布满弹孔和弹迹

总能多一道刻痕总还有十步可走 [1]

比利，你总是独行踽踽

他们说帕特·加勒特有你的号码

所以昏睡中也要睁一只眼

每个细小的声音都会是雷霆

是雷霆爆出他的枪管

你的结局会奏响在吉他琴

在图拉罗萨的某条小径

在佩科斯河谷也说不定

比利，你离家已经太远

总有新的陌生人在窥视

总有玩枪的傻瓜想身手一试

圣佩德罗总有老婊子要贴你

取你的精神取你的魂

---

1. 西部牛仔每击毙一人便在枪托上刻一道痕。以此曲配乐的电影中，牛仔们
须走十步，再转身射枪决斗。

陶斯的商人想要你完蛋
他们雇了帕特·加勒特与你了断
比利，要是死于你从前的伙伴
你会否被弄得太沮丧？

如果有个女人就守住她
记得在埃尔帕索有一个被你枪杀
她也许是个婊子，但她人很飒
比利，你跑出去已经太久

你的结局会奏响在吉他琴
在图拉罗萨的某条小径
在佩科斯河谷也说不定
比利，你离家已经太远

Billy

There's guns across the river aimin' at ya
Lawman on your trail, he'd like to catch ya
Bounty hunters, too, they'd like to get ya
Billy, they don't like you to be so free

Campin' out all night on the berenda
Dealin' cards 'til dawn in the hacienda
Up to Boot Hill they'd like to send ya
Billy, don't you turn your back on me

Playin' around with some sweet señorita
Into her dark hallway she will lead ya
In some lonesome shadows she will greet ya
Billy, you're so far away from home

There's eyes behind the mirrors in empty places
Bullet holes and scars between the spaces
There's always one more notch and ten more paces
Billy, and you're walkin' all alone

They say that Pat Garrett's got your number
So sleep with one eye open when you slumber
Every little sound just might be thunder
Thunder from the barrel of his gun

Guitars will play your grand finale
Down in some Tularosa alley
Maybe in the Rio Pecos valley
Billy, you're so far away from home

There's always some new stranger sneakin' glances
Some trigger-happy fool willin' to take chances
And some old whore from San Pedro to make advances
Advances on your spirit and your soul

The businessmen from Taos want you to go down
They've hired Pat Garrett to force a showdown
Billy, don't it make ya feel so low-down
To be shot down by the man who was your friend?

Hang on to your woman if you got one
Remember in El Paso, once, you shot one
She may have been a whore, but she was a hot one
Billy, you been runnin' for so long

Guitars will play your grand finale
Down in some Tularosa alley
Maybe in the Rio Pecos valley
Billy, you're so far away from home

敲着天堂的大门

妈妈，这枚徽章帮我取下
我再也不能用到它
天黑了，太黑了，我看不见了
感觉天堂的大门我敲着

敲，敲，敲着天堂的大门
敲，敲，敲着天堂的大门
敲，敲，敲着天堂的大门
敲，敲，敲着天堂的大门

妈妈，把我的枪埋进泥土
我再也不能朝他们开火
那道长长的黑云落下来
感觉天堂的大门我敲着

敲，敲，敲着天堂的大门
敲，敲，敲着天堂的大门
敲，敲，敲着天堂的大门
敲，敲，敲着天堂的大门

Knockin' on Heaven's Door

Mama, take this badge off of me
I can't use it anymore
It's gettin' dark, too dark for me to see
I feel like I'm knockin' on heaven's door

Knock, knock, knockin' on heaven's door
Knock, knock, knockin' on heaven's door
Knock, knock, knockin' on heaven's door
Knock, knock, knockin' on heaven's door

Mama, put my guns in the ground
I can't shoot them anymore
That long black cloud is comin' down
I feel like I'm knockin' on heaven's door

Knock, knock, knockin' on heaven's door
Knock, knock, knockin' on heaven's door
Knock, knock, knockin' on heaven's door
Knock, knock, knockin' on heaven's door

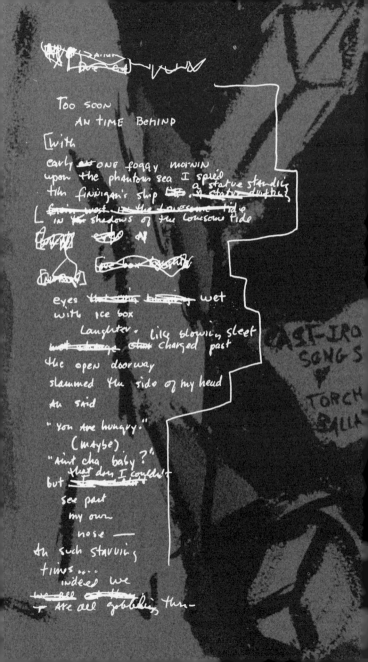

Too soon
an time behind

[with

early ~~as~~ one foggy mornin
upon the phantom sea I spied ~~a statue standing~~
tim finnigan's ship ~~be a statue drifting~~
~~from west in the lonesome tide~~
in ~~the~~ shadows of the lonesome tide

eyes ~~this song blowing~~ wet
with ice box
        laughter. like blowin sleet
~~wet storage snow~~ charged past
the open doorway
slammed the side of my head
an said

"you are hungry."
    (maybe)
"aint cha baby?"
but ~~that day I couldn't~~
see past
    my own
        nose —
th such starving
times....
    indeed we
~~we all at~~
+ ate all gobbling thru—

CAST-IRO
SONGS
♥
TORCH
BALLA

行星波
Planet Waves

周公度　译

　　《行星波》是鲍勃·迪伦破坏力潜藏的作品中少见的"温柔与哀泣之作"。在科学术语中，"行星波"意为由海底坡度形成的海底低频长波；暗潮涌起的变化，迪伦显然遥有感知。这张专辑由庇护所唱片公司发行于 1974 年 1 月 17 日，时值迪伦与萨拉的婚姻出现危机之际，因此被后来的传记作家与评论家重点分析。其中，《永远年轻》一曲传唱甚广，仅看章句，便会被那种青春激荡的情绪感染，结合他"游吟之音"的演绎，则更能体会出他的心意，那或许是对自己最小的儿子雅各布·迪伦的殷切期许。美国诗人艾伦·金斯伯格更认为"这首歌充满了希望，毫不玄奥，显然鼓励着人去找寻属于自己的真理"，"应给每个国家每所学校的每个孩子在每天早晨歌唱"。

　　忆念是整张专辑的情感底色。无论是《你身上的一些什么》的"五大湖的阴雨之日，走在老德卢斯的山里"，抑或《只除了你》的"常在墓地游戏 / 舞蹈，歌唱，奔跑"，乃至《永不说再见》

里描绘的冰湖、北风、海岸、钢铁，无一不是迪伦在回忆童年的家乡。此外，从《坚强的妈妈》《挽歌》偏灰暗色调的自剖，再到《婚礼之歌》那对妻子萨拉的表白示爱与忏悔告解，以上主题——组合，构成了第十四张专辑，一部讲述迪伦情感的"电影"。

周公度

在这样一个夜里

在这样一个夜里
很高兴你到我身边了
将我挽得这么紧
将一些咖啡渣加热
我们有很多话可说
有很多事堪忆
这确实是不错
在这样一个夜里

在这样一个夜里
很高兴你已过来留驻
挽住我，漂亮女士
说你绝不再远走迷途
你的手指滑过我的脊骨
带给我微微的欣喜
感觉确实不错
在这样一个夜里

在这样一个夜里
我无法入眠半分

外面空气这么冰冷

积雪又这么深

堆起火来，投进木柴

倾听它的嘶嘶

任它燃烧，燃烧，燃烧，燃烧

在这样一个夜里

将你的身体挨着我

一直伴我身旁

两人的空间够宽绰

就请别对我推搡

任四方的风吹打

在这老木屋门上

如果不是我离得太远

我想我们从前也曾这样

每多一个新的温柔之吻

就有更多的霜凝上窗玻璃

但感觉确实不错

在这样一个夜里

On a Night Like This

On a night like this
So glad you came around
Hold on to me so tight
And heat up some coffee grounds
We got much to talk about
And much to reminisce
It sure is right
On a night like this

On a night like this
So glad you've come to stay
Hold on to me, pretty miss
Say you'll never go away to stray
Run your fingers down my spine
Bring me a touch of bliss
It sure feels right
On a night like this

On a night like this
I can't get any sleep
The air is so cold outside
And the snow's so deep
Build a fire, throw on logs
And listen to it hiss
And let it burn, burn, burn, burn
On a night like this

Put your body next to mine
And keep me company

There is plenty a-room for all
So please don't elbow me

Let the four winds blow
Around this old cabin door
If I'm not too far off
I think we did this once before
There's more frost on the window glass
With each new tender kiss
But it sure feels right
On a night like this

走了，走了，已经走了 [1]

我刚到了一个地方
那里的柳树不弯垂
无需多言
这是尽头之最
我走了
我走了
我已经走了

我正合上这本书
合上书页和内里的文字
我并不当真关心
后续会发生何事
我就走了
我走了
我已经走了

我曾悬在绳上

---

1. 既是拍卖落槌时确认成交的提示语，亦是对棒球被击飞将要全垒打时的形容。

我曾坦荡正直

现在，我得割断

趁尚未太迟

所以我走了

我走了

我已经走了

奶奶说："孩子，去吧，循着你的心来

到最后你也会很好呢

不是金子都注定发光的

不要与你唯一的真爱分开"

我曾漫步在路上

我曾生活在边缘

现在，我得走了

趁未逼到悬崖以前

所以我走了

我就走了

我已经走了

Going, Going, Gone

I've just reached a place
Where the willow don't bend
There's not much more to be said
It's the top of the end
I'm going
I'm going
I'm gone

I'm closin' the book
On the pages and the text
And I don't really care
What happens next
I'm just going
I'm going
I'm gone

I been hangin' on threads
I been playin' it straight
Now, I've just got to cut loose
Before it gets late
So I'm going
I'm going
I'm gone

Grandma said, "Boy, go and follow your heart
And you'll be fine at the end of the line
All that's gold isn't meant to shine
Don't you and your one true love ever part"

I been walkin' the road
I been livin' on the edge
Now, I've just got to go
Before I get to the ledge
So I'm going
I'm just going
I'm gone

坚强的妈妈

坚强的妈妈，肉在你的骨头上抖
我要到河边捡些石头
姐姐在公路上和钢钻队一起
爸爸在大房子里，已过了要工作的日子
坚强的妈妈，我能在你面前抽会儿烟不？

黑夫人，你就不能把它挪开，腾出点地方？
稳稳地滚动，像一把扫帚扫过村乡
将你的双臂环绕着我，如晕轮之绕日
你有满满一口袋钱，但对我毫无助益
影夫人，你穿着一吨重的裙子

天使宝贝，生于变化之风与炫目之光
使我疯狂，你知道自己是谁，到过何方
盯着天花板，在椅子上站立
大火炽烈燃烧，灰烬空中扬起
天使宝贝，我想知道你在那儿做了什么事

我很沮丧——虚幻的世界就在我门口
我听到你在呼唤，一如往昔依旧

爬过草地，宛如兽穴中的狮子

前往彩虹的那一端聚集

坚强的妈妈，让我们上路吧，再一次

Tough Mama

Tough Mama, meat shakin' on your bones
I'm gonna go down to the river and get some stones
Sister's on the highway with that steel-drivin' crew
Papa's in the big house, his workin' days are through
Tough Mama, can I blow a little smoke on you?

Dark Lady, won't you move it on over and make some room?
Rollin' steady, sweepin' through the country like a broom
Put your arms around me, like a circle 'round the sun
You got a pocket full of money but you can't help me none
Shady Lady, the dress that you are wearin' weighs a ton

Angel Baby, born of a blinding light and a changing wind
Drive me crazy, you know who you are and where you've been
Starin' at the ceiling, standin' on the chair
Big fires blazing, ashes in the air
Angel Baby, I wonder what you done back there

I'm crestfallen—the world of illusion is at my door
I hear you callin', same old thing like it was before
Crawlin' through the meadow like a lion in the den
Headin' for the round-up at the rainbow's end
Tough Mama, let's get on the road again

黑兹尔

黑兹尔，棕金色的秀发
被看见与你形影相随我并不怕
你有我大为渴求的东西
噢，一点点你的爱意

黑兹尔，星尘在你眼中
你往某处去，我亦相从
我愿将天穹给你
噢，为了一点点你的爱意

哦不，我不需要任何提示
来得知自己究竟有多在乎
这不过令我盲目更盲目而已
因我到了山顶，你仍不在此处

黑兹尔，我随你的呼唤而至
如今不要让我玩这等待的游戏
你有我大为渴求的东西
噢，一点点你的爱意

Hazel

Hazel, dirty-blonde hair
I wouldn't be ashamed to be seen with you anywhere
You got something I want plenty of
Ooh, a little touch of your love

Hazel, stardust in your eye
You're goin' somewhere and so am I
I'd give you the sky high above
Ooh, for a little touch of your love

Oh no, I don't need any reminder
To know how much I really care
But it's just making me blinder and blinder
Because I'm up on a hill and still you're not there

Hazel, you called and I came
Now don't make me play this waiting game
You've got something I want plenty of
Ooh, a little touch of your love

你身上的一些什么

你身上的一些什么，划下火柴在我心里
是你举手投足的方式，还是秀发飘动的样子？
还是因为你使我想起了一些往事
横越自另一个世纪？

想来我已怀疑年轻时的幻影与奇迹
五大湖的阴雨之日，走在老德卢斯[1]的山里
我和丹妮·洛佩兹，冰冷的眼睛，漆黑的夜晚，后来是
　露丝
你身上的一些什么，唤起了久已遗忘的事实

我忽然发现了你，我的内心随之歌吟
无需再去寻觅，你是众多事情的魂灵
我可以说我会忠诚，可以用甜蜜轻松的口气
但那对你将是残忍，对我将是毁灭无疑

你身上的一些什么，趋时而优雅
昔日我处于旋风之中，如今则处境稍佳

----

1. 德卢斯，位于美国明尼苏达州，苏必利尔湖畔城市，迪伦的家乡。

我手按长剑，而你接棒继续

你身上的一些什么，我不大能明白指出

Something There Is About You

Something there is about you that strikes a match in me
Is it the way your body moves or is it the way your hair
  blows free?
Or is it because you remind me of something that used to be
Somethin' that crossed over from another century?

Thought I'd shaken the wonder and the phantoms of my
  youth
Rainy days on the Great Lakes, walkin' the hills of old Duluth
There was me and Danny Lopez, cold eyes, black night and
  then there was Ruth
Something there is about you that brings back a long-
  forgotten truth

Suddenly I found you and the spirit in me sings
Don't have to look no further, you're the soul of many
  things
I could say that I'd be faithful, I could say it in one sweet,
  easy breath
But to you that would be cruelty and to me it surely would
  be death

Something there is about you that moves with style and
  grace
I was in a whirlwind, now I'm in some better place
My hand's on the sabre and you've picked up the baton
Somethin' there is about you that I can't quite put my finger
  on

永远年轻

愿上帝永远赐福给你，保护你 [1]

愿你实现一切愿望

愿你总是为他人付出

也让他人给你帮忙

愿你搭一架梯子直通星辰 [2]

逐级攀登

愿你永远保持年轻

永远年轻，永远年轻

愿你永远保持年轻

愿你长大后能够公义

愿你长大后能够真挚

愿你总是晓得真理 [3]

看到光环绕你

愿你总是怀有勇气

立得正直且刚强 [4]

1.《旧约·民数记》6:24："愿耶和华赐福给你，保护你。"

2.《旧约·创世记》28:12，雅各梦见一梯子通往天堂。

3.《新约·约翰福音》8:32："你们必晓得真理，真理必叫你们得以自由。"

4.《旧约·诗篇》20:8："他们都屈身仆倒；我们却起来，立得正直。"

愿你永远保持年轻

永远年轻，永远年轻

愿你永远保持年轻

愿你的双手总是忙碌

愿你的双脚总是迅疾

愿你有牢固的根基

在风转向之际 [1]

愿你的心总是快乐

愿你的歌总被唱响

愿你永远保持年轻

永远年轻，永远年轻

愿你永远保持年轻

1.《新约·马太福音》7:24-25，聪明人将房子的根基立在磐石上，便不因风吹而倒塌。

Forever Young

May God bless and keep you always
May your wishes all come true
May you always do for others
And let others do for you
May you build a ladder to the stars
And climb on every rung
May you stay forever young
Forever young, forever young
May you stay forever young

May you grow up to be righteous
May you grow up to be true
May you always know the truth
And see the lights surrounding you
May you always be courageous
Stand upright and be strong
May you stay forever young
Forever young, forever young
May you stay forever young

May your hands always be busy
May your feet always be swift
May you have a strong foundation
When the winds of changes shift
May your heart always be joyful
May your song always be sung
May you stay forever young
Forever young, forever young
May you stay forever young

挽歌

我恨自己爱着你，以及由此暴露的弱点
你不过是自杀公路之旅中一张上了油彩的脸
舞台已经搭好，老旧旅馆四周的灯已熄
我恨自己爱着你，所幸落下了帷幕

我恨我们玩过的愚蠢游戏，以及表达过的需要
而你对我表现出的怜悯，谁又曾料想得到？
我离开了下百老汇[1]，但感觉仍置身那里
在那空无之域，殉道者哭泣，天使与罪嬉戏

听到你那些有关自由和永受剥夺之人的歌曲
当他的后背挨了鞭子，他便做出荒唐之举
像轨道上的奴隶，被打得直至驯服
都为了片刻的荣耀，那是肮脏朽烂的耻辱

有些人崇拜孤独，我不是其中之一
在这玻璃纤维的时代，我寻找一枚宝石
墙上的水晶球还没给我显出什么来

---

1. 下百老汇，位于美国田纳西州纳什维尔著名的乡村音乐街区。

我为独处付出了代价，但至少我没欠债

想不起你曾为我做过什么有用之事
除了在我跪下之时，拍了我的后背一次
我们凝视着对方的眼睛，直到一方回避
道歉是无用的，那又能有什么差异？

所以唱你的赞歌，关于进步，关于末日机器
无论何时能被看见，赤裸的真相仍是禁忌
照耀我的幸运女神，将告诉你我在哪
我恨自己爱着你，但我会克服它

Dirge

I hate myself for lovin' you and the weakness that it showed
You were just a painted face on a trip down Suicide Road
The stage was set, the lights went out all around the old
  hotel
I hate myself for lovin' you and I'm glad the curtain fell

I hate that foolish game we played and the need that was
  expressed
And the mercy that you showed to me, who ever would
  have guessed?
I went out on Lower Broadway and I felt that place within
That hollow place where martyrs weep and angels play with
  sin

Heard your songs of freedom and man forever stripped
Acting out his folly while his back is being whipped
Like a slave in orbit, he's beaten 'til he's tame
All for a moment's glory and it's a dirty, rotten shame

There are those who worship loneliness, I'm not one of
  them
In this age of fiberglass I'm searching for a gem
The crystal ball up on the wall hasn't shown me nothing yet
I've paid the price of solitude, but at last I'm out of debt

Can't recall a useful thing you ever did for me
'Cept pat me on the back one time when I was on my knees
We stared into each other's eyes 'til one of us would break
No use to apologize, what diff'rence would it make?

So sing your praise of progress and of the Doom Machine
The naked truth is still taboo whenever it can be seen
Lady Luck, who shines on me, will tell you where I'm at
I hate myself for lovin' you, but I should get over that

你，天使般的你

你，天使般的你
你以羽翼将我遮护
你走路与说话的样子
我想我几乎可唱出

你，天使般的你
你美好得像所有美好一般
你走路与说话的样子
确在我脑海里上演

你看我夜里始终无法入眠
这感觉以前从未有过
我夜里起床，在地板上踱
如果这就是爱，那么给我更多
更多更多更多更多

你，天使般的你
你美好非常
微笑的样子就像甜蜜婴孩
全投在了我身上

你看我夜里始终无法入眠
这感觉以前从未有过
从未夜里起床，在地板上踱
如果这就是爱，那么给我更多
更多更多更多

你，天使般的你
你以羽翼将我遮护
你走路与说话的样子
道出了全部

You Angel You

You angel you
You got me under your wing
The way you walk and the way you talk
I feel I could almost sing

You angel you
You're as fine as anything's fine
The way you walk and the way you talk
It sure plays on my mind

You know I can't sleep at night for trying
Never did feel this way before
I get up at night and walk the floor
If this is love then gimme more
And more and more and more and more

You angel you
You're as fine as can be
The way you smile like a sweet baby child
It just falls all over me

You know I can't sleep at night for trying
Never did feel this way before
Never did get up and walk the floor
If this is love then gimme more
And more and more and more

You angel you
You got me under your wing

The way you walk and the way you talk
It says everything

永不说再见

暮色在冰封的湖上
北风欲吹荡
在雪地上的足迹
底下是静寂

你的美丽难以形容
于我而言你很美丽
你可以使我泪溅
永不说再见

时间是我唯一所能给予
你可以选择拥有
你可以与我同居
永不说再见

我的梦想由铁与钢铸就
伴着一大束
玫瑰垂悬
从天空到地面

我站在沙滩
涌浪对我冲流
当时正等你的到来
抓住我的手

哦，宝宝，宝宝，蓝宝宝
你也会将你的姓氏改掉
你已把头发染成棕褐色
喜欢看它披垂着

Never Say Goodbye

Twilight on the frozen lake
North wind about to break
On footprints in the snow
Silence down below

You're beautiful beyond words
You're beautiful to me
You can make me cry
Never say goodbye

Time is all I have to give
You can have it if you choose
With me you can live
Never say goodbye

My dreams are made of iron and steel
With a big bouquet
Of roses hanging down
From the heavens to the ground

The crashing waves roll over me
As I stand upon the sand
Wait for you to come
And grab hold of my hand

Oh, baby, baby, baby blue
You'll change your last name, too
You've turned your hair to brown
Love to see it hangin' down

婚礼之歌

我爱你甚于以往，甚于时间与爱情
我爱你甚于金钱也甚于天上繁星
爱你甚于疯狂，甚于海上浪花
爱你甚于生命自身，你对我意义如许大

自从你径直走入，便得圆满
我告别了闹鬼的房间和街上的脸
还有小丑那个背阳的院子
我爱你甚于以往，而我还未开始

你对着我呼气，使我生活更为丰裕
当我深陷贫困，你教我如何给予
擦干我梦中的泪水，拉我出绝境
止住我的焦渴，满足我灵魂的炽盛

你给了我一个孩子，两个，三个，更挽救了我的生活
以眼还眼，以牙还牙，你的爱如刀割
我对你种种的牵挂，不曾休止，会把我宰了要是说谎
我会为你牺牲这个世界，任由自己的感官死亡

属于你和我在这世上奏起的曲调

我们会尽彼此所能去演绎，无论价值多少

失去的已失去，我们无以复得洪水冲走的一切

但幸福对我而言就是你，我爱你浓于血

再造整个世界素非我职

发起战斗冲锋亦非我意

因我爱你超过那一切，怀着一份不屈的爱

如果有来世，我爱你亦必复再

哦，你看不出么，你生来就是要站在我身旁

我生来就是要与你相伴，你生来就是我的新娘

你是我的另一半，你是我缺失的一块

而我爱你甚于以往，怀着不停歇的爱

你每天转变着我，教我双眼看见

待在你身边对我来说自然而然

而我不会让你离开，无论此后发生何事

因我爱你甚于以往，如今往日已逝

Wedding Song

I love you more than ever, more than time and more than
  love
I love you more than money and more than the stars above
Love you more than madness, more than waves upon the
  sea
Love you more than life itself, you mean that much to me

Ever since you walked right in, the circle's been complete
I've said goodbye to haunted rooms and faces in the street
To the courtyard of the jester which is hidden from the sun
I love you more than ever and I haven't yet begun

You breathed on me and made my life a richer one to live
When I was deep in poverty you taught me how to give
Dried the tears up from my dreams and pulled me from the
  hole
Quenched my thirst and satisfied the burning in my soul

You gave me babies one, two, three, what is more, you saved
  my life
Eye for eye and tooth for tooth, your love cuts like a knife
My thoughts of you don't ever rest, they'd kill me if I lie
I'd sacrifice the world for you and watch my senses die

The tune that is yours and mine to play upon this earth
We'll play it out the best we know, whatever it is worth
What's lost is lost, we can't regain what went down in the
  flood
But happiness to me is you and I love you more than blood

It's never been my duty to remake the world at large
Nor is it my intention to sound a battle charge
'Cause I love you more than all of that with a love that
    doesn't bend
And if there is eternity I'd love you there again

Oh, can't you see that you were born to stand by my side
And I was born to be with you, you were born to be my
    bride
You're the other half of what I am, you're the missing piece
And I love you more than ever with that love that doesn't
    cease

You turn the tide on me each day and teach my eyes to see
Just bein' next to you is a natural thing for me
And I could never let you go, no matter what goes on
'Cause I love you more than ever now that the past is gone

只除了你

这里没什么是我相信的
除了你，是啊你
也没什么对我而言以为神圣
除了你，是啊你

你是打动我的那一位
你是我钦慕的那一个
每回我们相遇
我的灵魂仿佛燃烧着
没什么我会在乎
也没什么是我渴慕的
除了你，是啊你

这里没什么是我着意追求的
除了你，是啊你
没什么是堪为之生或死的
除了你，是啊你

总在教堂之内
有首赞美诗我常听见

让我内心感觉如此美妙

如此平静，如此庄严

没什么能够令我记起那

钟声熟悉似从前

除了你，嗯啊你

常在墓地游戏

舞蹈，歌唱，奔跑，在我童稚之时

从不感到奇怪

但如今我哀痛地经过

那人间骨骸堆积之地

我知道有些什么已变改

我在这里是个陌生人，没人看到我

除了你，是啊你

没什么很可在乎或看似能取悦我

除了你，是啊你

没什么能催眠我

我也不为魔咒所陷

一切流经我

就像水出于井泉

每个人都希望引起我的注目

每个人都有东西要宣传

除了你，是啊你

Nobody 'Cept You

There's nothing 'round here I believe in
'Cept you, yeah you
And there's nothing to me that's sacred
'Cept you, yeah you

You're the one that reaches me
You're the one that I admire
Every time we meet together
My soul feels like it's on fire
Nothing matters to me
And there's nothing I desire
'Cept you, yeah you

Nothing 'round here I care to try for
'Cept you, yeah you
Got nothing left to live or die for
'Cept you, yeah you

There's a hymn I used to hear
In the churches all the time
Make me feel so good inside
So peaceful, so sublime
And there's nothing to remind me of that
Old familiar chime
'Cept you, uh huh you

Used to play in the cemetery
Dance and sing and run when I was a child
Never seemed strange

But now I just pass mournfully by
That place where the bones of life are piled
I know somethin' has changed
I'm a stranger here and no one sees me
'Cept you, yeah you

Nothing much matters or seems to please me
'Cept you, yeah you
Nothing hypnotizes me
Or holds me in a spell
Everything runs by me
Just like water from a well
Everybody wants my attention
Everybody's got something to sell
'Cept you, yeah you